FISHING WITH ANGELS

MARC DEGAGNE

To Claire

Three years ago, we stood in the kitchen
doing the dishes. Without warning, I told
you I thought I needed to write a novel.
You looked at me with your hands still
in the soapy water and said,
"Well then, write your book."
So I did.

Thank you for your loving patience with
my wild story idea.

"There are more things in Heaven and Earth, Horatio,

than are dreamt of in your philosophy."

~ William Shakespeare's *Macbeth*

FISHING WITH ANGELS

Marc Degagne

Recalling

Marie, my wife, passed ten years ago. Since then, it's become a tradition of mine to spend the first Sunday of each month with my son and his family. Although, driving over this Sunday, I feel more like a peasant on a pilgrimage than a father. My mind keeps travelling back on that journey to what happened years ago. I know what has triggered these long-forgotten memories—my boy recently purchasing a property along the same riverbank where it all took place. Without a doubt, after explaining to him what my fishing guide and I experienced, things will never be the same between us. Nevertheless, my account must be laid bare for my loved ones to judge for themselves. That's defiantly an excellent thing—no more secrets from the past.

I find myself squeezing the steering wheel, fearing cancelling the whole thing. But I keep driving on, determined. After all, this might help.

Let me give you a brief account before I pull into their driveway.

1975

It was supposed to be an ordinary weekend fishing trip like dozens before. But no, not that weekend. Without a care in the world, my old fishing guide, Astor, and I, walked along the trail parallel to the river. We found our spots, Astor a bit ahead of me, fishing upriver. While casting down river myself, at the first promising fishing hole, movement off in the distance caught my eye. I squinted, peering farther down the river, trying to determine the moving shapes. Was that … wolves? If so, and they carried along the way they were going, they would eventually have to cross our path.

As I studied the pack trotting along the bank, it never occurred to me to turn back. After all, we had a gun to scare them off with. Curiosity got the better of me. Blame it on my youth then, but I wanted to get closer to see what those wolves were up to. My decision on that sunny day altered my life in a way I could never have imagined.

I set off and went up to the edge of an escarpment that dropped a hundred feet to the riverbed. Even with binoculars, the wolves were so far away that they looked like drawn-out dots on the move. As they approached, making their way along the river, I marvelled at their agility, their ability to navigate such rugged terrain. Sleek bodies trailed each other in one area and then spread out, depending on how the wind blew scents their way.

Bold of them to travel through the vast open

country in the middle of the day. That indicated desperation, and a headstrong pack of wolves on the prowl was something to avoid. Astor and I should find a safe place to hunker down.

As I stood pondering the canine situation, my eyes caught something incomprehensible. Stunned, I blinked rapidly, trying to understand what I was seeing. "What on earth? What is that?" I whispered.

Two glowing beings stood above the tree line between the wolves and us, as you'd imagine them from the angels described in the Bible. I didn't know how to react to what I was seeing. I have no idea how long I stood there, heart throbbing, gaping at the sight, but I do remember the year, the day, and the hour, even though it's been decades. And every detail of what I saw is seared in my memory. How could anyone forget something like that?

Science would call it a phenomenon, the church, an apparition or a visitation from the divine. From the start, I expected the church to be supportive, lending an ear and laying hands on us to pray. At the other end of the spectrum, the good doctors of science would practice a more systematic approach if we shared with them what had happened.

I could imagine white frocks fussing about, sticking wires on my head and stepping back while scribbling on a notepad. I envisioned a doctor turning the dial on the contraption connected to my skull and launching inquiries such as, "Do you feel anything?" That would be about when I'd start craving coffee and want to go home. Unfortunately, the diagnoses wouldn't be dismissed that easily. The dedicated doctors would, no doubt, religiously press on to prescribe daily medication. Given time, the concoction would burn a hole in my stomach the size of Texas. But hold on a minute, not to grow faint and lose hope; doctors would have other pills to counter the side effects. Next thing I knew, I would have inherited a blister pack of colourful pills with convenient days and hours of the week inscribed on them, and I'd have to drink plenty of fluids and stay away from the sun.

If I had to decide between science or the church, I'd choose to be prayed over with perhaps a cup of herbal tea.

Anyway, I digress. Back to the angels. If you haven't dismissed my experience as some psychotic episode, here comes the crazy part. As I stood there, still shaken and staring wide-eyed at the angels, the thought drifted through my head, *is this what you experience after you're dead?* Somehow, I found the courage to do something. Slow stepping and cautious not to make any noise, I walked closer, not even thinking about Astor and what he might be doing.

Hunching my back in an attempt to hide beneath a bushy pine tree, I eased my body nearer to the angels. With trembling hands, I pressed the trusted binoculars hard around my eye sockets, re-focusing the lens in a frenzy. My teeth wouldn't stop chattering. I felt grossly inadequate to approach them but unable to stop myself, and I did manage to get closer to my subjects, the angels.

Pouf! A raven flew across my view in a dark flash. Panic surged through me, and I stumbled backward, barely managing not to fall onto my backside. My bent ankles held the sudden weight shifting, but just. Somehow, I still clutched the binoculars in one hand. The other was braced against the pine tree trunk to steady me. "Shush," I hissed at myself as if that would help my situation.

Long grass rustled behind me, and I glanced over my shoulder. Astor reached me and crouched at my side. He laid a firm hand on a shoulder while whispering in my ear, "You were not to see this so soon. Change of plans, Joe; the wolves got in the way."

I stared at him, barely comprehending what he was saying. Astor knew about the wolves? And the angels?

He nodded as though he'd read my confused thoughts. "That's why the moose is down there, see?". He pointed through the trees, in the direction of the divine beings, with a wedged hand. "You and I need to go down there, meet with the angels and ask what's going on."

I jerked my head, still gaping at him. "You knew all along about the angels, Astor?"

"Yes, the angels, but not the wolves or moose. That pack of wolves is a stick in the wheel, my friend. But don't worry Joe. My meeting with the angels was planned, and I'm sure they can take care of the wolves for us. I can explain everything later." Astor let go of my shoulder and gave me a firm slap on the back that I suppose was meant to be reassuring. I didn't feel a thing other than my insides dropping. I swallowed hard. The wolves were getting closer; I could hear them.

I didn't want to go down there where they were, not just yet.

Present day

There, now you have an idea of what I'm dealing with. I forget if Astor pointed out the moose before or after I saw the angels. Either way, it doesn't matter. As you can imagine, it's not a topic a person can discuss with family and friends without some preparation. Especially on a Sunday morning after church with my grand-daughter running around. On this bright Sunday though, I believe I am finally prepared. The time has come to disclose my grandiose, once-in-a-lifetime experience of some forty-nine years ago.

Still, I have this weird sensation that it won't be easy. Since I got out of bed this morning, my fingers can't find rest. They keep rubbing each other as I wrestle with my thoughts. A question comes creeping to the surface, not with audible words but a feeling deep in the pit of my stomach. *What will they think?* Last night, as I tossed in my sleep, my heart also spoke to me. *Take a step back—don't go there.*

But what if I find the courage to do so? Over and over, the question reverberates through my mind: *How will they react?*

Way Up North

I park next to my son's attached garage and get out of my truck. The sun warms my shoulders, and I look up and breathe deeply. Perfect weather. I cup my hands against the door window at the side of the garage and peek inside. No vehicle. A glance at my wristwatch confirms my suspicion. Oh, right, I'm an hour early. The whole family is still at church. That happens when you're eager to get something off your chest.

As I wander towards the back of the house, whistling, relief fills me. This is an excellent opportunity to walk down the river and explore where the wolves congregated many years ago. The backyard has been mowed recently, and long grass has parted at the lawn's edge where the trail leads toward the river. Finding a discarded walking stick, I crouch to pick it up and stroll along the path, still whistling. In northern countries, it only takes a light breeze to feel ice curling around your neck. At this time of year, the forest undergrowth, being sparse, adds little protection. I suspect the cool river contributes her share of chills in the early summer.

I trek further along the beaten path, thrashing the underbrush with my newly found stick. At the same time, I keep an eye out for the skull or jawbone of that moose that could still be half buried in the soil. After so many years, I know I am looking for a miracle. So, I ask myself, who would've prophesied that I, Joseph, would stand on this particular riverfront forest at the location where heaven intervened some 49 years ago? Was this arrangement a coincidence or divine planning, my son Finnegan purchasing a home with 30 acres along the same stretch of the river? I doubt it was an accident. As I walk around and stand for a while, pondering the situation, a chill rippled through my legs, and my knees ache from balancing on uneven ground. Even so, I want to persevere in my investigation.

"Hello, Dad?" The crisp morning air carries my son's voice like a town's church bell. Has one hour passed already? The timber is sparse from where I stand. He must have spotted me between tree trunks and called out from his backyard. I try to answer my firstborn by looking towards his house, although my voice fails me. This is a good time for a hot cup of courage.

"Wait, give me two more minutes of serenity in the woods, if you please." As I turn back to look over the river, the same tall boulder from 49 years ago appears between the trees. I'm about to walk toward the water for a closer inspection when I hear leaves rustling behind me. The unmistakable footsteps dragging dried rubbish draw closer. My son has grown weary of calling out without replies and is closing in fast. This is it, my friend; the moment has arrived. I take a heavy breath, knowing an avalanche of inquiries will follow.

"What's going on, Pops? Why are you walking around in the woods in your fancy shoes?"

I feel sheepish and ill-prepared. While staring down at my footwear I muse, Joe, you should have worn army boots to tell your story, not Sunday shoes. For a split second, I get sidetracked. But hey, no rest for the wicked. More questions roll out from my son like bullets from a machine gun. We're French; it's in our DNA.

"Did you see a bear at the river, Dad, or a moose? You look pale; are you cold? Did you take your medication this morning?"

His last remark rubs me the wrong way. Why is it that when people get older, they must take some medication to stay alive? I am insulted and show it with a smirk. My son sneaks in a crooked smile before surrendering with a peace sign. Right, he got me. Even so, that deserves a slap in the ribs, which I administer. Useless! It's like hitting a stump, prompting loud laughter without showing an ounce of respect. Forget it; back to the angel story.

I swallow hard. Like panning for gold, I travel up the creek for this one. With a steady hand, I point toward the riverfront. The whole exercise feels like lead. "Look!" I say in surprisingly a firm voice. "Look at that tall boulder sticking out in the middle of the forest. How did it get there? In God's creation, how did it manage to crawl over there?"

Outwardly, I am Samson in the Bible; inwardly, a pack of nerves. The moments of silence between us feel like an eternity. When I jerk my head up, my boy is looking out to where I am pointing. Like a back-row student, he stretched, unconcerned, both arms in the air. Then he yawned, displaying a full set of teeth. Finally, after exhaling the rest of his disruptive yawn, Finnegan answered.

"Ice," he said briskly. "The ice age did that. A deposit, leftovers from when the river was frozen and much higher at some point in our history."

I cut him off before his scientific mind could elaborate any further.

"No," I said, "the angels moved it." There. I said it in plain language; there's no turning back now. And, by the way, this is part of the story I have not mentioned yet, the boulder moving, travelling back in time to 1200 A.D. But I will, you wait, back to my son's reaction. He stands motionless, close to my side. A dreadful silence hangs around us, broken only by heavy breathing. I know his body has turned to face me, but I don't respond.

Under the circumstance, standing still and staring toward the river is more convincing. Stay focused and hold on; tension should ease in a minute; talking and reasoning will follow. My firstborn is a quick thinker. He's got eyes in the back of his head, and he's not easily fooled, being a schoolteacher. I don't have to pretend. And I don't need to look; on hold is a frown with folded arms poised to hear a further explanation. Being thrown into a different dimension from this world can be a struggle for mature Christians, never mind new believers. His face holds an air of openness with a tint of concern. Phew! So far, so good.

"Why would angels go around moving boulders in the wilderness?" said Finnegan.

We're on a roll. Without missing a beat, I answered somberly, "They did it to prepare a smooth path for the moose."

My son turns to look at me, more profoundly this time, and I don't think he is conscious of his hand pointing a finger in the woods as he announces, methodically, "You don't need smooth trails in the forest for a moose to walk on."

I come back in the same tone, "This one needed it. The moose had an accident hours before. His hind leg broke, snapped right in half."

We wide-eyed each other like deer in headlights; then his voice rises dramatically. "What are you talking about, Dad? You're not making any sense."

A standstill. It's my age, you see. He grants me a few precious seconds of silence to assemble my thinking, to take a deep breath to steady my story. Thank you, son.

"It happened a long time ago. You weren't even born yet; I was single."

Another pause. Even the birds have fallen quiet. The tension in the air is thick enough to slice and make a sandwich, but I plow ahead anyway. "I have never forgotten that summer day; who would? The angels, my old friend Astor and I were fishing together. Son, I'm counting on you to listen with an open mind. After, you can throw me in the loony bin if you want; I don't care. My story should only take an afternoon at best if you want to hear it. Do you have time?"

I get all this out before he interrupts me. "Hold on! Stop right there. How do you know they were angels and not aliens from outer space?"

What a question; the answer is obvious. I quickly slam shut my son's presumption. "Because none of them walked around like zombies. They were majestic, tall with thick shoulders and strong looking."

My son jumps in with both feet. "They? You saw more than one?"

Now he's on overdrive. I answer evenly, "Yes, two."

While his body leans away from me as though he might catch whatever I have, his voice holds an air of amusement. "Which one moved the boulder?"

I take his question seriously. "I don't know; the two of them did. They were looking towards the boulder and back to the moose in slow motion; they must have used psychokines or something." The professor's meticulous English comes through.

"You mean psychokinesis."

I nod. "Yeah, whatever."

Without warning, my son's arms flew out, fingers wide apart, as though he needed to slow our wild conversation down, breathe, and think. "Moving a boulder in the woods? What for?"

I raise my voice to clarify precisely why the boulder moved. "I told you to make a path for the injured moose. O yeah, wolves; a pack of hungry wolves were part of the excitement." At this point, I know that, out of respect, my son withholds comments that might diminish the other person's point of view. I love him more when he does that. A soldiering snap of the chin, and he speaks again. That's my boy. "Okay, Dad," he said as an open hand went up, patting the air, and he repeated, "Okay, Dad, start from the beginning. In what period of your life did this occur?"

"That summer, over 49 years ago. You were—"

Without excusing himself for interrupting, the boy crashes in like he often does. "Dad! Dad! Get to the story, will you? Wolves, angels."

Disturbed, I raise both hands in protest. "This *is* part of my story," I say, "how I got there before the wolves and the angels. Anyway, let me tell you what triggered my decision to discuss the encounter, It's your house with the acreage along the river that you, Mister Finn, purchased last month. Yes, right where we're standing. Is this a pure coincidence, or what? Heaven knows. Remember that birthday weekend last month when we piled into the truck? You said you had something exciting to show me. We drove to this place, and Diane let me pull the sold sign off the front lawn. On our way home, Diane got so excited; she couldn't stop talking about the heated workshop for her pottery. A flood of memories stirred in me that day. I never intended to talk about it. With all the years that have passed, I thought the angel had forgotten, but he didn't, or they didn't. I was reminded a few days ago in a dream. The voice said, 'The time is at hand; pass it on.' That's why I'm responding to that call. After praying about it this week, I've decided to take a step of faith. The angel gave clear instructions. 'Go ahead, unleash that heavenly purpose.' The shorter angel repeatedly told me loudly, 'So to enhance the Kingdom of God!' So, here I am, declaring for the Kingdom of God."

I study my son's six-foot frame for a sign of hope, feeling completely defenceless, as though I'm standing before a judge ready to hammer *guilty*. Somehow, I don't give a hoot. "You think I'm crazy, don't you? Well, don't you?"

Finn's arms are crossed high on his chest like a bouncer. Thank God the school strap has been banned. His empowering body posture was a cover-up, as he answered like a nurse in a maternity ward. "If you want to get something off your chest, Father, I'm here to listen; the day is ours." He used the endearing *Father's* name; the lad is deadly serious. Then he has the gall to repeat, "We may need another look at your medication."

Look at my medication. A more civilized way of saying I might be losing it. I shrug. Sounds reasonable to me; I can live with that. But first, I am going to tell my angel story.

Telling

"**R**emember the old fishing guide, Astor? Probably not, as you were gone, teaching in the big city when he passed away. We went fishing one weekend years ago, just the two of us. If you wanted to catch lots of fish, Astor was the man to be with. I recall getting up early that Saturday morning, fishing gear already packed on the floor from the night before. We planned for him to pick me up at my house with his truck; it was simpler that way since Astor knew the roads like the back of his hand. I chipped in for gas. The air was cool that early summer morning, so I waited indoors for my ride. Besides, I had a good view from my living room window. I had no idea that my life would hit a crossroads that day. Ignorance is bliss, they say. I didn't know we'd almost get killed in a moose accident on the road, get stuck, encounter a mean bear, or face a pack of wolves, for that matter. Let's not forget the angels and our travels in the sky. Also, that strange raven always hanging around is beyond me."

Whoops! I was interrupted by you know who.

"Wait, let me guess what you experienced, Dad."

"What for?" I say, surprised.

"Just for fun, let me try and guess," says Finn. With the palm of his hand cradling an elbow, Finnegan's fingers went tapping white teeth, thinking, clearly excited for the moment. His eyes narrow, and he speaks in a longing voice, detailing what I might have seen.

"Your eyes could hardly believe what lay before you, Dad—a pack of wolves and a majestic moose lying together in a lush meadow. The sound of birds fills the air. High up in the sky, a flock of geese flies peacefully in a *V* pattern."

Both hands flutter in the air when he comes to the last part. I am concerned; is he losing it or just making fun? Who knows? I cannot help but frown in silence, but I keep calm and listen more.

"O yes, and then, in the background, your whole body, mind, and soul immerse themselves in soft, angelic music, singing, 'Joy to the World'!" A boyish face with a wide grin turns to me, nodding. I'm pretty sure my eyebrows stick out more than usual. With a disappointed look plastered, I huff and gawk at him. Still, he wasn't catching on. The innocent smile on my son's face broke. "So, am I close?"

I show no mercy. "No."

His youthful countenance collapses along with the shoulders; head hung in silence like a grade two pupil spilling the wrong answer.

"Okay, I give up; what happened, Father dearest?" Now he's grasping for restoration, that son of mine.

Without finesse, I answer in plain English, "The

wolves ate the moose." For some, a pack of wolves devouring a moose can be perceived as brutal, but that's how nature works.

Blood drains from his cheeks. My answer physically takes him aback. "Whoa!" he said. "That doesn't sound like an angelic atmosphere, especially for the moose."

You don't understand," I said. "You weren't there."

"Yeah, I wouldn't want to be standing in the middle of it all fishing."

Okay, the boy is taking too long. With both fists stuffed in my jacket, I must launch two strides forward and come back sidestepping. I'm standing knee-deep in the middle of it all; time to forge ahead with my story. I answer, racing, full of words. "No, I can guarantee you wouldn't want to be fishing with wolves nipping at your heels. May I continue now?"

"Yes," said my son, "but sorry, not here. That north wind is cutting through my sweater like razor blades. Let's head for my living room with a civilized thermostat on the wall to continue our conversation comfortably. Meanwhile, I can lend you some socks; you need to do something about those shoes, Dad. They're all worn out."

As we walk towards the house side by each, our voices echo in the woods. His shoe remark triggers my thinking of newer footwear, which forces me to stop and lift one leg to have a look. Ouch! Au contraire. My Sunday shoes are good for another five years. "By the way, those socks you'll lend me are probably mine from last summer when you fell in the creek."

"No, they're not," Finn protests.

"Yes, they are."

"No, they are n-o-t; I don't buy knee-high argyle socks, Dad."

That sounds like parental abuse, which I resent, so I have no qualms slashing back, "What is wrong with argyle socks? At least mine cover past the ankles."

He laughs. "Forget it; I have all kinds of socks for you."

"Okay," I say. "As long as they cover close to my knees."

"Why do you need extra-long socks? You wear long johns year-round, don't you?"

"Yes." I bow graciously in response to his inquiry. "I stay warm all year in compliance with the Northern Province lifestyle. Hello, the Yukon."

My son responds by laughing out loud, arms wide apart. As we head for the house, we debate everything under the sun. If anyone had been watching at a distance, they'd have seen the arms of father and son flailing like two maestros gone ballistic. Looking back, I can confidently say I won the main argument that day.

Working Angel

An angel speaks. "Humans will never lay eyes on the mystery left behind 49 years ago, God forbid. Joe and Finn had casually walked by it that morning like cattle grazing in the field—not a clue, as is so often the case with human beings. Right there, at the old cedar stump along the trail, halfway to Joe's son's backyard. Only I, Joe's guardian angel, know that the evidence remains—a low-lying contour covered in mounds of grass from countless wet seasons.

Its shape confirms something other than wood, other than vegetation. The clipping sound of rock hard material gives it away. Clip, clip, a nuthatch perched in the arch formation sharpens his beak on the oval surface. The precious spot is worn to a yellowish-white groove. The tiny bird has performed this task daily since early spring to maintain the tool of his livelihood, a razor-sharp beak—clip, clip. From a distance, the object looks like the chewed hand of Bigfoot sticking out of a swamp. Until now, it's been a record-dry summer; the river is low. The forest floor draws a clear picture. Certain wetland shrubs couldn't handle the abrupt change and dried-up dark brown. Others thrived. The ecosystem presents itself as a mosaic of earth-brown at ground level to forest green on top. Clusters of pitted tamaracks grew sporadically like hydro poles in the last century. Along the way, the trunk obscures its crown with a mishmash of thick, interlocking branches. The ever-present green smears the background like plaster. Round purple hills are left behind the river, set against a cloudless, blue sky. Rest assured, by the end of the summer, from various shrubs thriving, a multitude of fruit berries will hang by the handful, the target of countless flocks of birds. God's provision for those facing the autumn migration comes through, all the time.

The ivory structure of an old moose antler preserved in acidic mud had recently been exposed. The same moose that the wolves devoured 49 years ago. A clan of wood mice arrived weeks ago. The skittish, bulgy-eyed rodents dug elaborate burrows and chewed the antler in the darkness below the surface, out of sight of predators like owls. The moose rack began to disappear, the antlers sinking into the mud as they nibbled. The mice will leave no trace behind except empty tunnels and droppings. In nature, the good times in finding a nourishing treasure are short-lived; therefore, nothing goes to waste—clip, clip.

Rest assured, the red squirrel will visit later, scrounging for bits of antler. She, too, has craved calcium in her milk. And the neighbouring porcupine is hiding during the day in a bushy hemlock. Watch out, if Porky discovers the rare antler prize before it is gone, the rodents' burrows will be trampled, and the remains of the moose rack eaten in a week. Like all rodents, monsieur porcupine also yearns for calcium supplementation.

So, Joe and his family will never discover the large antlers sinking into the mud. They will be eaten and remain a mystery.

Inside the House

Along the trail to the house, Finn runs in front of me and goes indoors. Minutes later, I stand with a bent knee on his stairs before stepping onto the deck. After walking across cedar boards, I cautiously step over a little girl's bike left crashed in front of the door. That reminds me of Finnegan; he used to do the same thing.

As I reach for the doorknob, I feel a coolness in the palm of my hand. With a huff, I turn sideways in the doorway, take one last breath of cool air, and scan the distant river before entering. From an old habit of mine, I remove my cap as I walk in. I can hear pots and pans clamouring in the kitchen with gospel music playing in the background. My daughter-in-law Diane is on some sort of mission impossible. I've learned fast not to get in her way or ask questions about her cooking.

Finnegan had bolted inside ahead of me minutes before for a reason. To announce that I had been found alive and well at the river. I suspect he gave a short account of our angel conversation. Lower back pain cries out for me to sit down before we continue our talk where we left off. Also, my toes ache for dry socks to make matters more urgent. Still, I hesitate before shutting the door behind me. Oh, how my soul longs to drive home for an afternoon nap. Too late. Diane wraps her arms around my shoulders in a bear hug, followed by smacks on the cheeks. Exclamation mark! Exclamation mark! French culture.

Acting jubilant with raised hands, Diane doesn't ask permission to greet people in the doorway lavishly; the bear hug lingers. I have no choice but to feel grateful every time. Excessive greetings boil over as if we haven't seen each other in three years. I never could keep up with Diane's inquiries about well-being. We separate at arm's length, although she still holds my wrist and chants, with her beautiful smile, "How are you, Joseph?" She means every syllable.

While enquiring, she leans her head to one side, nodding. It takes a bit of convincing, but finally, she accepts that I'm doing fine. Like magic, motherhood has eyes to see through doors; without looking behind her, she raises her voice while pointing at the door and saying, "Lillian, please put your bike away."

Most endearingly, Diane is like a bloodhound regarding relationships. She can detect family and friends blocks away and will eventually close in to embrace and kiss them on both cheeks like a true Frenchman from France, even with a stampede of relatives dropping in on Christmas holidays. To avoid a commotion, I sometimes step aside in the foyer and walk in discretely; she will track me down. Thank God some traditions never change.

My granddaughter Lillian wakes up from her nap and comes crashing into my arms. "Grandpa! Grandpa, you're here."

"Yes, sweetheart, I'm here." I crouch to pick her up, knees cracking, chest huffing. "Oh my!" I say. "You're growing again."

"Did you see something at the river? Are you taking me fishing, Grandpa?"

I pat her back. "Not today, princess."

A frazzle of curly blond hair brushes my face with a light scent of bubble bath soap; it tickles. My snow princess demands, "Carry me on your shoulder, Grandpa. Carry me, please."

"I will," I whisper with a wink, "but first, you better put your bike away."

She does, and, in seconds, comes flying back inside, door slamming—this time, Diane overlooks giving her instructions on how to shut a back door.

Lillian's brisk excursion of putting her bike in the garage gives me enough time to squat, take my shoes off, and place them on the rubber mat. I toss Lillian on my left shoulder and stomp around the living room announcing, "One sack of potatoes for sale, one sack of potatoes for sale, five dollars."

With arms and long curly hair flailing behind my back, she screeches with delight and is to be rescued, pronto. Her busy mother walks absent-mindedly across the living room to open the curtains and then casually returns to the kitchen without looking back. Finnegan is bent over, poking at a log in the fireplace. Both parents ignore her pleas. I grasp her chubby knee with one hand and swing her into my arms. Inches away from the couch, I let her flop on her backside among soft cushions. Her hair is a mess. She closes her eyes, pretending to have fainted.

I laugh. "Faker."

A pair of large, blue eyes instantly appears. "No, you are."

I ignore her reply and call her a weasel.

She points her buttery finger at me and says, "No, you're a weasel." I draw back, pretending to be hurt and distraught. She laughs out loud at my demise while pointing her finger in my face once more. Suddenly, her mother calls for help in the kitchen, and my feisty granddaughter sits straight on the couch. Jumping to her feet, she flashes a regretful smile before running to help her mother. Rest assured, she'll be back for more challenges.

My son's voice drifts out from the kitchen. "Is it my turn to make lunch?"

Her response was like a busy nurse in a war zone, precise and without fuss. "You took too long to find your father," she says. "I already made lunch. The roast beef for supper is in the slow cooker.

I make my way to the doorway and stand, where I can witness what is going on in the kitchen. Diane straightens. "Really," she waves a hand for emphasis, "I'm fine; go in the living room." With a mother's instinct, she shifts her attention to her daughter.

"Careful, sweetie. The stove is hot."

As I head for the reclining chair, my toes are slowly drying. I can't hear all of it, but Finnegan pulls Diane aside in the kitchen, whispering. They are discussing my angelic encounter and, most importantly, whether they should include Lillian when I share the story.

They call for me to join them for lunch at the kitchen island. Squash soup with cheese on sourdough bread is on the menu. We eat and agree to avoid the angel story until we're all done and sitting in the living room.

And, finally, we are. Finnegan makes his entrance with a tray of homemade cookies, the ones that stick to your fingers. Diane sits on the couch with Lillian on her lap. She is eight months pregnant and more beautiful, more radiant than ever; a little girl (my own personal prophesy, 8 pounds-4 ounces). The new arrival will bring plenty of joy into their lives.

First things first, we deliberate possible weather conditions for the week, the month, and the year like all Canadians do when they meet. People say our weather in the Yukon is like politics—give it a few hours, and it will change to freezing rain, hail, or a foot of snow.

Diane had brought in the coffee pot to complement the tray of homemade cookies. She appears to be as anxious about the angel story as a midnight fox circling the chicken coop. We have decided that my granddaughter can stay in the room. Young children like Lillian are natural candidates for receiving miracles and angels and stories about heaven; none of us are concerned. Diane is a new Christian on fire. She isn't saying much, but a quick flash of her brown eyes exposes her thinking; she wants to be part of my angel encounter.

I am thrilled by her interest and love her the more for it. Diane opens a child's storybook to conceal a notepad, while cuddling with Lillian. Out of respect for the queen of the castle, no one says a word about her book being upside down. Tropical plants decorate all corners of the living room like an oasis, which makes you forget about the darkness and the long winters in the Yukon. One shrub alone stands six feet tall, planted in an old copper wash tub that bears succulent citrus fruit year-round, imagine that.

The sizable windows invite the outside scenery in without the cold, which makes it surreal. Their main bay window faces a distant pond with waterfowl flying in and out. I assume that, when holding a cup of coffee in the morning and looking out, a person could deliberate life to no end. Oftentimes, at sunrise, Finnegan has witnessed herds of animals grazing unperturbed only some twenty yards away from the house.

My son sits on the couch across from me, leaning forward with bent elbows resting on his knees. His head hangs low as he gently caresses a coffee cup in the palm of his hand. Small talks like weather inquiries and the local news are spent. Two pairs of knee socks are neatly folded on the sofa next to him; I was right, he did borrow some. Still, how thoughtful of him to wash and return them.

Okay, it's time for the rest of my story. I press my shoulders back to sink deeper and find the side lever, which pushes my legs up on a padded footrest. The set-up is like lying on clouds, almost in heaven. I take a deep breath and wave a hand to the side, hopeful it will help me fall way back in time, to 49 years ago. Then I open my mouth and let my words flow without holding anything back. I begin to explain in detail the rest of my encounter with the angel fishing and the wolves and my visit to the year 1200 A.D. and everything in between.

Fishing

It started innocently enough, going fishing for the day with my friend Astor. I didn't realize then that, that same afternoon, my views of the world we live in would take a dramatic turn. As a practicing Christian, embarking on a personal relationship with the Divine changed my life forever. How could it not? Thereafter, I realized that my life on this earth was one time, one race, and forever in a thousand other dimensions.

"It was on these premises where it happened, Finn, on your 30 acres that run along the river. I was living in town back then. I stood inside the house that early morning, watching through my living room window. I recall as clear as day being impatient, waiting for Astor to pick me up to go fishing. I specifically remember being captivated by a bumblebee on my living room window. I stood scrutinizing the insect's movements to pass the time before leaving. The tiny bundle kept running into the glass, confused.

What strange behavior for such a small creature. I thought back then. How odd. That blatant glass wall—the obstruction was there for all to see. Although the reasoning in his little world told him that there was nothing to stop him, his sense of touch told another story. In many ways, the nature of bees to harvest honey and navigate back to their hive is much more advanced than humans; still, the bee's abilities fell short in this state of affairs. His curved body shook in frustration, exhausting him physically and mentally. The buzzing was surprisingly loud for such a tiny, yellow creature.

My concern growing, I couldn't turn away. A struggling honey gatherer desperate to get free is pitiful to witness. A comical dance, an unusual and troublesome performance. It seems that nature is ill-equipped to deal with manmade circumstances, those not found in the ecosystem. I couldn't help but wonder, is it the same for us in the spiritual world? Are we well-equipped for heaven's ecosystem? Do we respond the same in our little world as a bumblebee on a windowpane? Sensing a clear, infinite expanse on the other side, waiting for us with open arms? If only we could have a breakthrough. Bumping into the transparent wall, with our deeds, our words.

So often, when living our lives on this earth, we Christians labour to grasp the eternal. We apply the same technique over and over, expecting different results; isn't that the definition of madness? For some of us, the struggle ends with much disappointment. Why are we so prone to fear, to doubt? According to the Word of God, the door of grace is always open; we can leave all cares to Him and come in.

Anyway, about that time, I started to speak out loud

to the bee, as if we were old friends. "Easy now, big fellow. Attempting to shatter glass with head butting is fruitless, Mister Bee. Right you are, we do have something in common. We both have a longing to be forever free and fly on wings like eagles. We both desperately need help beyond our wildest capabilities. For me, it's my God. And for you, my stubborn bee, a giant will do."

I placed the bottom of a large drinking glass in the palm of my hand and pressed the rim to the window, trapping the distraught bee. Pinching a piece of thin cardboard in my other hand, I carefully slide it between the rim and the window to establish a top lid. Then it was time to flip the drinking glass upright, taking care to hold steady pressure on the lid with my fingers. Even though the disoriented bee wasn't hurt in the process, his protest escalated; he wanted my head. The close-quarters buzzing got on my nerves. I constantly shook the glass to keep the bumblebee at the bottom so that no attempts would be made to sting me through the paper lid.

He kept flying to the top; it was like dealing with a juvenile delinquent. It had to be done quickly. I swung around, arms outstretched as much as possible to keep the container away from my body. At that point, I'm quite sure I was making a not-so-brave face. I took two giant strides, heading for the door. In the fresh morning breeze, I gave freedom to my housebound bumblebee of questionable behavior. I did not expect any acknowledgment in return.

"I never knew about you buying a house in town," said Finnegan.

I nodded. "Let me tell you a bit about it."

The House

"That spring, after six months of renting, I purchased my first home in the city of Whitehorse. Within a week, your father, the prodigal, made plans for the future and was more driven than ever. The location was simple to pinpoint. I always preferred the southern section of town, as the area was elevated with mature trees and large backyards. As far as I'm concerned, houses with covered front porches and huge backyards felt warmer, more connected. How else would you be able to sit and wave at your neighbour walking by? And how to know if old mister so and so was out walking his dog? Since the house interior was outdated and without a full basement at the time, I got a smashing deal."

Lillian stirs in her mother's arms and looks up at her. "Stop, wait for me," she says. "I have to go pee."

My princess races towards the bathroom before Diane can say, "Well, go sweetie. Hurry!"

The bathroom door slams shut. Minutes later, a flushing noise. We all wait patiently and smile at each other.

"Don't forget to wash your hands," bellows Diane.

A faint, "Yes, Mom," filters through the wall, and we listen to a child's commotion when sliding a footstool across the floor to reach the faucets. I take a sip of coffee while waiting and then sink my teeth into a soft cookie. As I do, I happen to turn my head to look outside. Yards away, a porcupine is strolling across the lawn. It isn't that unusual or threatening, I reason; they don't have a pet dog. A raven perched high up in the trees is squawking. With a blank look, I stare in the general direction of the large black bird. Is it the same one? I shake my head. Not possible; they don't live that long.

This time, the little princess's feet bring her rushing into Finnigan's arms. She asks if she can have another cookie and colour. (Now you know who's the softy.) Finnigan and Diane set Lillian at the coffee table with her colouring books. Seated on the floor, legs crossed, elbows out, Lillian is ready to go.

Finnegan has a puzzled look on his face. Raising a finger, he asks what I concluded was important for him to know. "Explain to me, Dad," he said, squinting his eyes, "how did you manage to convert a crawl space into a full basement?"

"Good question," I said. "Let me tell you." I continue like an old college professor who knows his stuff like the back of his hand.

"After digging the inside, the concrete step was exposed, which defined the footing. That's where I laid my cement floor. I raised the house three feet with hydraulic jacks, adding three rows of cement blocks. I ended up with a basement just over six feet; I'm 5 feet 9 inches, so I was happy with that. At the time when all this was going on, I thought to myself, you're in the Yukon, young man; get a combination wood and oil furnace. So that's what I did. For cement block walls, I used a sledgehammer to punch out the basement door. The back doorway, which was connected to the woodshed, turned out to be the most used entrance. No more trekking outside in the middle of winter to get wood. My electrical skills started by running wires from the main panel to the shed. Of course, for home insurance purposes, I had a licensed electrician connect everything and give his stamp his approval. By doing most of the work myself, though, your father became a true handyman.

"Starting on my own in a new city, I had no choice but to learn fast, stuff like working with power tools, and using first aid. I dove into house projects like a fish in water. I must admit, the energetic jack of all trades wouldn't have survived without help from my neighbours, Jack and Alfonse. Alfonse, a retired sub-contractor for residential homes, was awesome. He possessed practical knowledge that can't be found in books. His daily quote was, 'Set-up is everything.' Coffee breaks lasted a minimum of half an hour for the old gentlemen—the first 15 minutes warm-up or cool down on warm summer days along with life stories that rarely repeat themselves.

"I cherished the abrupt instruction from Alfonse's

no-nonsense set-up and his insistence on doing things right the first time. His words were never meant to offend. After having a working crew for 20 years, being in charge came naturally. Occasionally, he'd remind us all that, 'Time is money; let's finish this'."

"Jack, on the other hand, classified himself as the aggregate specialist. He did wonders with wood fencing, decks, and landscaping. With good Christian intent, only once did I mention I could pay for their help. I got the silent look of reproach in return. I regretted raising the topic and never mentioned it again. In the following years, I was able to return the favor by helping to renovate their houses. I learned quickly in my younger years that when you give without expecting in return, one way or another it always comes around.

"The previous owner of my place had left an old caribou antler that had seen better days bolted to the shed. A bird had built a nest inside it, and since the birds might return to it, I did not have the heart to tear it down. Somehow it seemed the old caribou antler had squatters' rights to my backyard shed. The front porch facing the road had a sloped roof attached below the second-story window. Broad cedar frame windows allowed a panoramic view of my street. The enclosed front porch offered ample space for a comfortable armchair. My feet could easily stretch out to a footstool. The coffee table next to my chair accommodated the trusted fly swatter and coffee mug. Your father sat there on many occasions, contemplating the remains of the day. After bagging my first moose one fall, I celebrated by smoking a big cigar on that porch. An hour later, I puked my brains out, which canceled that tradition in a hurry. The whole porch-cabana structure stood winterized and heated making it usable year-round."

Oops! I'm detecting a conspicuous yawn from Diane. My home renovation exploits are dragging her attention to numbness. Lillian has rested her head on her folded arm on the coffee table, one eye open. I am losing my audience. How can I spike the girl's interest? Ah, yes—the story of how I met her grandma.

My wife, Marie, passed away ten years ago, but Lillian still perks up with interest whenever I mention Grandma. So, I lean forward, still sitting in my chair but with a cupped hand to my cheek. In a secretive voice, I ask my granddaughter, "Princess, would you like to know how I met your grandma years ago?"

She lifts her head from colouring and, with a wide smile, whispers back, "Yes, tell me, Grandpa."

"I don't know the story, either," Diane pipes -up.

Finnigan's head is hanging low, but he's smiling fondly, one arm around Diane. He was only 14 years old when his mother died. I lift both arms in a 'V' and exclaim, "Well then, my Princess, ladies, and gentlemen, let me tell you." I shift a little in the recliner, getting comfortable, and then begin my story.

"Lounging on my front porch is precisely where I was, contemplating the remains of the day with coffee at hand, when I saw your grandmother for the first time, my Princess. She was a beauty. At the time, we were, of course, both oblivious to the fact that we would fall in love in the future; that took time and commitment on Grandpa and Grandma's part, let me tell you.

"I'd been sitting comfortably, leaning back in my armchair for a while, assessing the plans for the next day. My coffee was getting cold, and I was about to call it a night. Across the road in front of Grandpa's house, the popular porcupine trail wove through town. Nothing was paved, only hard-packed gravel with cement pillars at the road crossing to allow bicyclists and pedestrians with dogs to access the runway. In the evenings, I saw plenty of locals walking through. From inside my porch, if I spotted white rows of teeth with a hand waving, it meant *hello, a neighbour* with a grin. Although the evening glare on my front windows could sometime obscure visibility, I always nodded anyway and waved back, guessing, who? What? After being in the neighbourhood for a time, I couldn't help but take notes like: *I haven't seen Mister Smith walking his dog this evening, I wonder why?* or *I never saw those two before* or, *Here comes that attractive girl walking with her dog again. Wowzers!*"

I go stone silent and lean forward to whisper the name *Grandma* for Lillian's benefit; she pokes her head up from colouring and smiles, nodding yes, yes, go on. Satisfied, I continue.

"Her schedule always seemed to coincide with my evening sitting on the front porch. A healthy, cheeky face with wavy brown hair, that one. She turned towards my house to wave and offer her alluring smile. That evening, the pretty lady tugged at my heart, although her greeting was stiff and brief in motion. Her other overburdened arm was stretched out in front of her like a rope. The 10-foot leash traversed the trail, zigzagging from one side to the other. A dog, tongue hanging out, was attached to the other end and appeared determined to sniff every inch of soil.

"The pretty girl held on to the leash for dear life. I remember taking a drawn-out sip of lukewarm liquid, thinking, and rethinking. As men tend to do, I made practical, mental calculations, trying to solve the problem. Out loud, I asked heaven a profound question, 'Why do small people routinely adopt canine companions they could ride like a horse?'

"She was petite, the dog humongous, a massive Great Dane. A breed of dogs the Vikings used for war to eat huts with the people inside. I don't want to sound cynical, only I could visualize, one fateful day, a red squirrel scooting across the trail in front of the Lone Ranger's dog-horse. The following day, I'd read in the local paper, right on the front page: 'Horrific discovery! Bloody leash with attached forearm found in the woods! Caucasian.' Nah, I canceled that dreadful thought. 'Careful what you critique,' my mother would say. 'It may end up in your lap'."

"That's exactly what happened, Princess. You see, that petite lady blossomed to be your father's mother, your grandma. I even let goof head lick my face, simply to impress her. The next year we got married. Soon after, I converted my shed into a doghouse. For Christmas festivities, the old caribou rack hanging on the outside shed would fit perfectly on the goofy dog's head. But your grandma frowned on that idea."

Diane laughs out loud, and Finnigan grins shamelessly, ear to ear. Lillian perks her head up and asks cheerfully, "Did you walk the dog, Grandpa?"

"Oh yes," I say. "I walked the dog numerous times." I point my finger at her before adding, "But I refused to pick up anything with a plastic bag." Drawing a line in front of me, I add, "The buck stops here"

Lillian and Diane draw their heads back and laugh again and again. I smile at my granddaughter; just like her mother, that one.

What a person doesn't endure when in love.

Going Fishing

I still recall that fateful morning like it was yesterday. I remember walking in circles while fussing over my fishing gear. "Where is my ride?" I nervously finger-combed my hair over my ears at every turn. Already 6 am. Pacing back and forth gave the impression that I needed to use the washroom badly; I didn't. Confined inside, in front of the window, drove me insane; the old grandfather clock tick-tocks like a time bomb. The coffee pot is empty. I started second-guessing the plans we'd made the week before. Had Astor said 6 or 6:30?

I got irritated with myself for not calling the night before to confirm the rendezvous time. That sounded much too civilized. Communication could be sparse when supposed grown-up guys arranged fishing trips on the fly. They ended up with inquiries downstream at the fishing spot like, "Did you bring any water?"

At ten minutes past 6, a human shadow appeared at the end of my driveway. Yes, finally! I didn't need to see his face; the whole-body posture gave the man away. Astor is a short, thick, barrel-chested man with rounded shoulders from years of portaging. Even when Astor stands relaxed, his forearms always hang bent at the elbows. Like Father would say, "A 45-gallon drum filled to the brim is not an easy thing to tip over, nor would you want to." With hands cupped close to his thighs, the man appeared ready to draw in a high-noon gunfight. His upper body tended to lean forward when walking, which gave the notion that his next step would be to crouch and pick up supplies. And not under any circumstances could bushy eyebrows succeed in hiding his prominent schnozzle. Last but not least, he always had a toothpick stuck in his mouth and, oh yes, the hat.

Astor attempted to straighten his body with little effect; he waved at the window with his bear paw and then turned to walk away. What would be the rationale for walking over to the door, knocking, shuffling, and declining to enter? and exchanging pleasantries when we had a two-hour drive? That would be Astor's explanation for not coming to the front door and wasting valuable fishing time.

That was the signal, the hand waving. I swung back on both heels and then bent forward to grab my fishing gear. I slid an arm through the strap of my backpack and hefted it onto my shoulder. Almost simultaneously, I grabbed my professional case-in fishing rod with my other hand.

Straightening, equipment in hand, instinct made me pat my shirt pocket to make sure the sunglasses hadn't slipped out. That quick body movement left me a bit dazed in the head. No problem. I took a deep breath to shrug it off. Okay, I had everything. I hoped. Several giant strides got me to the front door. As soon as half my body was extended outside, my cheeks were instantly soothed by the cool, fresh morning air. I paused and swiveled back to stick my face inside, still gripping the doorknob. *Hurry, focus, and take a second inventory.* All lights out except one, coffeemaker off, the thermostat on low, side door secure, yes, fantastic. Let's go fishing! Click.

For me, a 4x4 pickup truck with oversized tires required a mountain climbing technique to get in. I started with a high-five hand reaching for the door handle, then grabbing and pulling. After placing my left foot flat on the floor mat, I had to use both arms to haul myself up. Concentrating like an athlete on rings, I hoped to land with dignity. Now perched on one cheek at the edge of the seat, I needed one more sitting adjustment, and, voila! I was in the cab with the truck door left wide open. All the while, the neighbour's dog barked steadily. He wanted to come too. Not to help matters, my driver stared straight ahead, drumming his fingers on the steering wheel. I grunted to let him know that, with cumbersome fishing equipment, I was hustling as fast as I could. The door creaked when I slammed it shut. Instantly, the whump of air pressure inside muffled the dog barking. Every time I do this, I feel like I'm saddling up on a horse. Although, embarking on a two-hour drive in a reclining chair minus the wood lever can't exactly be compared with the wild west. On second thought, I'm glad I'm not on a horse. No doubt, we're going fishing in style.

I spoke, breathing heavily, not looking at my friend. "Good morning, Astor. How's your week been?" In my peripheral view, I saw Astor nodding, the toothpick sliding from one corner of his mouth to the other. Get this, when driving with his sunglasses, my guide looked like one of those people who lent money at 80 percent. The outback Australian hat with a clump of partridge tail feathers tucked to one side sealed the deal.

"Good morning, young man," said Astor. "Did you think I'd forget to pick you up?" His right eye quivered, betraying humor.

My hand went up in protest. "No, no. I knew you'd show up. I've never known you to be late."

Without acknowledging my reply, the chirping went on. "You look a bit pale, didn't sleep well last night?" He waited for a response with pursed lips, assuming the obvious.

This man Astor comes across as an individual with few words, content to live on the inside. A lifetime fishing and hunting guide. Getting up at dawn before others, evolved into second nature. After hanging around with Astor for a while, I started noticing valuable living habits such as how to make yourself comfortable when enjoying the outdoors. The guy conserves energy like a monk and does not waste any time when moving around the campsite. His every body movement has a purpose, a goal, and a work plan to accomplish specific tasks. At the same time, I was subjected to the humorous side of him. He created a pleasant atmosphere filled with skills of the outdoors mixed up with crazy stories. It made life interesting, to say the least.

Looking back at the hat with partridge feathers sticking out, umm, the only sensible observation I could make while sitting in that truck was that Astor needed to go out and shoot another bird. The outback brim with the depleted partridge feathers swung around as he backed out of my driveway. That allowed me to examine his jacket of numerous portages. The fabric had stretched to match his thick shoulders ages ago. The broadside pockets and two front ones were worn thin and stretched out, presumable from carrying stuff when working outside.

I could envision the old scout making his tours along campsites, sprucing them up for the season, talking with campers about safety, and reporting any wrongdoing. Astor possessed a steadfast responsibility when it came to excommunicating previous campers who'd strewn trash around the campsite. He condemned the practice like an old-time preacher slamming the pulpit. There would be hell to pay! More than once had I witnessed Astor's frustration with people. Agitated arms would slice the air like a swordsman in the heat of battle. He, voicing retribution, would, I guarantee, have prompted St. Peter to act.

"Who wants to walk on pristine shorelines and see a pop can stick out of the sand? Who?" Astor would cry out. When thunder rolled, lightning would strike. Envision sitting in the truck with Astor, head hung in reverence. I, the listener, wholeheartedly supported the preacher's principles and added *amen* to that sort of ruling whenever it came down.

A sudden acceleration forced my shoulders into the seat of the truck. My heart quivered with delight. The neighbour's dog gave up barking. I stared through the windshield, longing to arrive soon at our fishing area. After examining Astor's jacket while backing out of the driveway, I felt a bit disappointed with myself. I patted the shirt pocket not holding the sunglasses and glanced down with a sour face. *Why is my shirt pocket ironed flat to my chest?* I looked like one of those young guys advertising men's shirts in the Eaton's catalog. I needed to get outside more and build things. I promised myself that when I got back from my fishing trip, I would go out and buy more tools.

I hummed as we commenced driving out of the city, although, even though daylight had arrived hours ago, my body was still adjusting to the early rise. I felt a sense of equality, as though I belonged, as we drove northwest; I supposed being human was what you made of it in your lifetime. After stopping at the third and last red light, we abandoned the city with gusto. I didn't know about Astor, but I needed a hearty breakfast to curb the expectancy in the pit of my stomach. A roast beef sandwich with mustard on whole wheat bread clutched in one hand improved the situation.

Arriving from the big city not long ago, I'm still constantly surprised that it doesn't take long to leave a small town; one last Tom's coffee shop sign, and pouf!

civilization vanished. Giant pines flanked the road on both sides. Twisting my head up against the side window, I marveled at the steeples of pine forest spread out, measureless, beneath mountainous skies. A growth of giants displaying the absolute—the forest dominates this region. The scenery captured my soul in a minute and didn't let go. For centuries in the Yukon, we've known that as the call of the wild.

I remember that morning clearly. I felt light-headed, with no deadlines in sight and no worries. I was completely conscious of my surroundings. With no heavy loads on my shoulders, walking over mountains felt attainable. I let myself drop the past and shut out planning the future. I, your father, sat in the speedy truck basking in the present.

Unbeknownst to me, that one day would forever transform my perspective on life on earth. Who are we humans that heaven appoints angels to intervene on our behalf? Like the ancient prophets in the King James Bible would cry out, "Who am I, Lord? Choose someone else." Many times this week I awoke perspiring, frantic. What to do? What to say? How do you respond when reminded after so many years? Do you hide incredible knowledge under a rock or shout it out on mountaintops? I, your father, was entrusted with living words of tremendous value, a treasure box that can never be emptied. We all have choices to make. The fool, the fearful, flings away the lot and walks away, absent-minded. I prayed for the courage not to change my course nor distance myself to a journey elsewhere.

Take Jonah in the Bible as an example. At first, the God-fearing man Jonah decided to hide and run the other way; look what happened to him.

As we traveled along the road, a wall of jack pines blocked the morning sun. Although, beams of sunlight occasionally broke between tree trunks, creating pulsing sunrays that exploded in my face. The bombardment of pure light threw me off guard for a minute. In pain, my head jerked backward, eyes shut. The sting! Unstoppable tears rolled down my cheeks. But I didn't mind the warmth, and the lesson was learned quickly. I swung the truck's sun visor over to the side window and peered through the front windshield; nonetheless, I still felt the heat rays palpitating on my temple.

My sense of smell helped me daydream about salmon sizzling in butter. The pretend smoky aroma filled my nostrils, and the excess saliva made me swallow. My stomach knew what I was thinking about; it responded with a trail of gurgling noise. My beef sandwich had been eaten much too fast. Thinking about the vastness of the Yukon made me glance at my backpack, lying on the floor mat. On purpose, I nudged the pack sideways with my knee to catch the faint sound of contained liquid splashing around. Wise planning, including coffee in my repertoire.

"The thin strap holding the binoculars against my chest pressed against the back of my neck. Yes, a worthy companion in open country. The tackle box and fishing rod were an obvious presence. No need to think about an extra pair of dry socks—that had been arranged two years before in a sealed Ziplock plastic bag and secured in one of the outside pouch compartments. Waterproof matches, fork-spoon combo utensils, and a fillet knife with an attached leather pouch for a sharpening stone completed my fishing trip supplies. All we needed now was the fish, and to keep an eye out for bears. We drove ten minutes in complete silence. All you could hear was the engine humming and the frame rattling as the front tires hit the occasional pothole.

"I felt the urge to start another conversation, so I did. "Looks like we're gonna have a good day for fishing, Astor."

As if absorbing my prediction in a breath, Astor's shoulders rose as he nodded in agreement. At the same time, the toothpick shifted from one side of his mouth to the other. That was when he spoke. "Yep. Apart from pouring rain, any day is a fine arrangement for fishing." After a scrupulous glance, he asked, "Got everything you need in that pile, Fin?"

I answered like a front-row student. "Yes, sir. I double-checked it was all there." I'd known the question would eventually surface—Astor was a fishing guide to the core, constantly concerned about adequate supplies for the road. For Astor, a planned trip cut short due to a lack of substance is like a thorn in the flesh. His face will hang, grumpy, for hours. He can't hide it anymore; I've figured him out. The pro woodsman plans for extra supplies in emergencies, but he never lets on that he has more unless needed. From experience, I knew he would let me hang in dismay for a while. So, I'd learned my lesson and never wished to repeat the words, 'I clean forgot' on one of Astor's fishing trips.

After my tormentor was satisfied that I'd dangled from a rope long enough, he would casually toss the forgotten item in my lap with a grin. Instant joy, phew! I'd quickly express my gratitude. "Thank you, Astor, you're a lifesaver." Another lesson learned.

Thumping a hand on the steering wheel, Astor grunted and then glanced towards me. "I forgot to ask you; we could've stopped at Tom's coffee shop back there."

My absent-minded arm lifted in protest. "No, no, there's no need, Astor. I packed my large stainless-steel coffee thermos with lunch. Thanks, anyway."

The sun rose higher. With my forehead glued to the side door window, I was absorbed in viewing grandiose landscapes rolling by like an old movie script, although in full colour. Only the classical song 'Born Free in C minor' proved to be absent; my imagination made up for that. Like families in tight communities visiting regularly, I'd become familiar with Astor's colourful character; it grew on you. His most interesting habit was the famous, die-hard toothpick. Although, for the life of me, I could never pinpoint which pocket held the box of toothpicks.

Like clockwork, when Astor possessed a new train of thought, his upper body jerked back, followed by a head bob as if needing to agree with himself before speaking. Last but not least, the toothpick would switch sides with a flick of the tongue. That theatrical maneuver grew deeper and more elaborate with each of his old stories. Oh! Mercy me. On rare occasions, they'd come around twice.

In the past, while sitting in his vehicle with my seat belt fastened like any law-abiding Canadian, I thought of bailing out. But, traveling at a bone-fracturing speed, that was not an option. I had no choice but to perk up, show interest, and listen.

The theme song 'Born Free' playing in my head was interrupted by Astor popping a question. "How's work been this week, Finn?"

The question felt foreign to my ears as if the intruder spoke German. My mind fought back, wanting to stay with the lion running along the river. Even turning my head towards him didn't help—I couldn't answer right away. Instead, I thought about what it was like to stand alone and peacefully in the middle of a forest. To me, a forest is like someone playing a fine instrument; walking by, it makes you stop, not wanting to leave. It has no walls, no doors to shut you out or in. Like eternity, a forest makes you feel ageless. Now why would anyone want to leave?

I finally came out of it, still groggy but recovered enough to acknowledge my chauffeur. "Oh fine," I said, "except things turned ballistic on Tuesday morning. I got slapped across the face once and spit at twice. I moved out of the way for the spitting. You can always see the spitting coming." I turned to witness a face grimacing, crow's feet spreading on cheekbones.

Astor's tone revealed his concern. "What happened, some fellow forgets to take his medication?"

The response to that inquiry alone would be a three-day seminar—immeasurably complex for a one-sentence answer. I lifted a defeated hand next to my ear. Shifting in my seat, I felt like a cornered animal. I responded to Astor's troublesome question by saying, "I don't know. It was just one of those days, a full moon, some say."

My driver stared straight ahead, pondering that with a sour face. That was when I decided to be frank with my enquirer. "If it's okay with you, Astor," I said, almost pleading, "I want to forget about work and concentrate on going fishing."

The atmosphere turned dead silent. For a minute, I thought perhaps I was being rude and had stepped over the line. Then he shifted his body, stretching both arms out from the steering wheel, he pushed himself back tight into the seat and eagerly agreed with *yes* head movements. I could tell that he regretted bringing up the whole work-week subject. What was he thinking, breaking the golden rule of not talking about work on a fishing trip? With a 180-degree turn in conduct, Astor plowed ahead. "Great idea," he said. "Let's do that. Ah-hum! Did you hear the wolves howling last night?"

The wolves? After scratching a body itch, it took a few seconds for the question to register. "No," I said, curious. "I sleep like a log. Where did it come from, along the river?"

Oops. The toothpick slid to the other corner of his mouth. This was destined to be a profound explanation. Astor pointed at something through the windshield, added silence for authority, and then spoke. "With mountains and open valleys around us, it's hard to tell; the echo factor bouncing across reports strange locations to the human ear, plus the wind and fog muffles distances. If someone asked me to guess, I'd say it sounded like they made a fresh kill south of town on the other side of the river."

Perfect, that was where we wanted them; they don't like crossing open water and getting soaked to the bone. Where we're headed to go fishing right now, the river is wide and fast flowing. Only a forest fire closing in on the riverbank would make a wolf jump in and swim. Hey! The weatherman called for cloudy all day; that was a blessing—the watchful salmon wouldn't see our shadow in the shallows. We had an hour of paved road ahead of us, except for the last mile when we'd turn eastward, and, after parking, hike half an hour upstream, tracing the riverbank.

Upriver a short distance, the landscape rose a hundred feet with the river splitting in two. Right in the middle of that fast-flowing current lay an island, an outcrop of tangled boulders covered with studded growth—an ideal nesting environment for kingfishers, Astor always said. I loved to watch them dive underwater to catch fish. And, as Astor reminded me that day, "Let's not forget, Joe, that famous kingfisher bird is stamped on our five-dollar bill. It's known to be a bountiful sign when you see one coming out of the water with a fish in its beak."

I pondered that in a fog, not answering my fishing partner, hoping that it wouldn't kick off another of his pioneer stories about kingfishers. Phew! Wonderful; Astor continued without missing a beat.

"Formed by the fast flow down the river, deep pools are gouged just past the island by a tamed current swirling back on itself. The big fish naturally swim in circles at the bottom to escape the relentless currents and rest. When swimming around in deep water, they don't have to worry about bears. For most bears, they're almost beyond their reach, and it costs more valuable energy to go after them than it's worth."

I'm guessing that the older, experienced bear must reason by instinct, that there is plenty in more hospitable water.

"On my mother's grave," declares Astor, "it's a prestigious spot to hook a big one. If you don't mind skipping class, Joe, and getting educated in a hurry, we can always start there."

That made me smile. When Astor took you fishing, he didn't hold anything back. You learned to appreciate his expertise, and his kindness, along with any sporadic ego brawls. Although, it struck me after he described the location, that Astor had never taken me fishing in that area before. I should have realized then that this trip was going to be different.

I turned to look outside once more. On both sides of

the road, beyond shallow ditches, an army of gigantic conifers monopolized the area. The green corridor with tops penetrating blue sky narrowed to a point on the road ahead. The highway in front of us simply disappeared in a 'V' at the next curve and the next. Nature continually swallows pavement along with city life and its clamour.

For a time, neither of us spoke. The absent of utterance felt meaningful. We were two individuals at peace with our surroundings, content to reminisce on a road less travelled. Far and wide, I viewed the spectacular scenery in comfort. I thought at the time that this was truly a land marveled at by locals and tourists and angels alike. After absorbing the constant humming movement in my ear, I caught myself, conscious of my head drooping; drowsiness was seeping in. The skin on my forehead felt cool where it was pressed against the side window—a good position to relax neck muscles and look out at the same time, a good place to bat an eye and dream. Beyond the glass, the south side of a mountain with no name sloped down at 30 degrees on all sides; that was no dream. Centuries ago, gigantic boulders had cascaded down its flanks to congeal with Mother Earth. Hardy shrubs had taken root in crevasses amid poor soil, casting precious shade in otherwise open country. A heartfelt visiting place for mountain goats on the move.

For miles, the foothills ran jaggedly as if traced with colourful crayons in a child's fist. In deep ravines, slivers of dwarf growth faced nearly impossible conditions—stony and freezing cold. After heavy rains, a mountain creek rushes down the middle, splashing white over rocks. The dark, irregular stepping stones in the mix testified to centuries of washouts. My eyes caught a black smear in the sky above. Now and then, dipping a wing for correction, the lone raven flew with a purpose—he was trailing up and down the white-water stream. The large, black bird had good reason. He hoped to detect a four-legged creature that had slipped and got injured or died. Observing the raven soaring in his daily survival technique to exploit the unfortunate felt special.

From the road, my eyes fell on a figure standing way up on the ridge at one of the lookouts. The tall individual was leaning forward, his chin resting on the butt end of a walking stick he'd cushioned with his hands. The high-noon hiker had paused to ponder and rest. Cocked on one leg, the other foot rested securely against the side of his knee. For us traveling along in the truck, it appeared that the person could just as well be standing on a dune in the Sahara Desert.

For greater effect, scavengers circled high above his head. By the trousers, he looked like a German tourist. Even driving by on the road far below, I felt a kinship for what the lone hiker experienced up on the trail.

With my temple pressed against the window, I managed to glance upward, ahead of us. A smoky white cap loomed, painted in blue-grey. I didn't have a clue what was going on up there. I could imagine blankets of snow retreating from warm summer rays, a constant, multicoloured mist bound for heaven. Awesome, the mountain remained shrouded all year long. Only mature eagles were capable of soaring through the mist and witnessing the summit up close.

The mountain vapor blended in with the purple, orange, blue, pink, and red in a thousand different shades stretching across the sky. With surrounding atmospheric currents, the sky was constantly mixing, and shifting. I had time to take a half-drawn-out breath of wonder before the scenery carried on to the next picture frame.

Grandpa

A glance towards Astor, and what? The toothpick appeared shiny in his mouth. I'd missed it again —the rare maneuver of Astor taking a new one out. The toothpick moved between his lips, from the east to the west with one flick of the tongue. You could count on it; out of nowhere, a story was about to unfold, and heaven and earth could not stop it. First, I heard a deep breath, his shoulders rising. Then the unmistakable head nod to acknowledge the absolute in his story. The orator opened his mouth with no fear of the toothpick falling on his lap. With fond recollection, Astor started to speak matter-of-factly.

"Have I ever mentioned the story that my mother told me when I was a young boy?"

I froze, silent, until it felt awkward, and then blurted out, "No."

That was the only reply Astor needed to take off running. On your mark, get set…

"Well, it's a true story about my grandfather coming back from the First World War. Like all war experiences, separation ran rampant, loss of loved ones, pain, and suffering. Beyond all that, my grandfather's story evolved into something beneficial; circumstances shifted at the end with great hope for humankind." A pause? "Please bear with me, Joseph, and I will tell you my story." Astor's open hand patted the air between us, asking for patience.

I sat bracing myself, stiff neck with tight lips, looking straight ahead. I would be dragged along without my chauffeur caring if I could bear it or not.

Without missing a beat, Monsieur bent on storytelling, added. "This is how I feel each year around Christmas time; I get the sense that I'm standing at a crossroads for a major turnaround, and there's hope for the future."

I know. We're months from the Christmas holidays. Astor's stories have no barriers to time, and he doesn't care. To help his thoughts go back to the Great War, Astor's hand rose to his ear, waving time away as if shooing a fly. It looked so weird that I turned to see if something tangible was happening. In a breath, Astor's mouth parted, the toothpick glued to the corner of it, and the saga continued.

"When my grandfather, on my mother's side, came back from overseas…" Long pause. "You should know, his name was Monsieur Armand Charbonneau, that's French. From his arrival back to Canada, the father of three acted reflective and somber towards friends and family. My grandmother, Arc-Ange, noticed the abrupt change. Grandpa didn't want to talk about the war. Not unusual for most soldiers. Back then, people wanted to forget the war and simply go on with their lives. After a short time back home, though, it didn't matter much. His decisive behavior exposed Grandpa's true sentiments about the great battle. My grandpa performed three specific tasks after returning. First, he bundled up all his military clothes, shirt, pants, and undergarments, and carried them into the backyard to the burning barrel. He poured gasoline on them, struck a match, and burned the lot, fleas and all, with a wide grin on his face.

"Second, for the rest of his life, while living on the farm, Grandpa Charbonneau never allowed guns to enter his home and never again went hunting either. None of his hunting friends and relatives made any remarks or faulted him for taking a stand against guns. But it was the third thing that Grandpa did that was a bit odd, somewhat out of character. And this is where the story turns with some hope for humanity. So, again, please bear with me, young feller, and I will tell you the rest of my story."

The open, pleading hand went up in mid-air again. I remained seriously mute with bulging eyes looking straight at him. He didn't appear to detect my nervousness; I was invisible. Wonderful, our driver was blind, and we were going to have a wreck.

Le raconteur continues. "What my grandpapa did a few days after that was extraordinary." Pause. Astor's right hand went up to flag the coming climax so that he would not be interrupted. I had no intention of disturbing such a determined creature. Astor's elevated voice continued. "The third unique chore my grandpa performed on that fateful day was this: one morning, he stood in the middle of the kitchen, holding his military helmet with both hands. He stared at it for a while, and then he turned it over.

"I'm sure that Grandmother was eying his every move with curiosity. My mother was seven years old back then; being a tom-boy, she preferred working outside with her papa. On that day, she was sitting at the kitchen table, also watching her father with interest. *Why is Papa holding the helmet in his hand?* she thought, with furrowed eyebrows, and a thump in her chest. *Does he want to go back to war?*

"Mother and daughter both observed the back of Papa's suspenders as he walked to the front porch. He set the helmet on the porch and then returned to the house without a word. Behold, after supper that same evening, Papa heaped food scraps on a pie plate, strolled to the front porch, and scraped the contents into the war helmet he had left on the porch. Yep! From that day on, my grandfather used his helmet as a bowl to feed their dog, Buster. Hey! It wasn't a bad idea. Every year around Christmas time, I think about what my grandfather did. And I hope that one day all the armies of the world will go home for the last time and the soldiers will use their helmets as bowls to feed their cats and dogs. If you sit back and think about it," exclaimed Astor, "it's not a bad plan."

With his left hand holding the steering wheel, Astor raised his free arm as though holding an imaginary bowl in his hand. A thin voice escaped between tight lips to produce an animal call. "Here… kitty kitty kitty."

Unbelievable! During the moment of silence that followed, my pillar of salt posture held, my eyes hinged left and then right without me turning my head. Finally, my head inched towards Astor, and ah… I managed to say something meaningful. "That's interesting; is it true?"

The scruffy character with the outback Australian hat had crow's feet spreading out from his temples declared, in the name of St. Peter, "It's nothing but the truth, so help me, God." The booming smile plastered on his face was obvious—Astor was proud of what his grandfather had achieved.

At that point, I was at a loss. I didn't know what else to say, but I'm a survivor. By scratching the left side of my neck, I managed to create a little distance from my possibly out-of-balance companion, Astor. I pressed my shoulder flat against the truck's door to lean away even more. Rubbing my lower lip with two fingers helped to accumulate precious time. Hopefully, my driver friend would think I was pondering what he had just revealed. In any case, Astor didn't feel obliged to interrupt; only waited. Was he expecting more of a reaction to his story? I honestly didn't know how to respond. Keep looking forward, I thought. This too will pass.

On the Road

"I'm on the road again!" A hit country song came rolling on the radio. Perfect timing. I could feel my insides lifting to ramble away. I never wanted that song to end. "I just can't wait to get on the road again." With my left foot tapping the working people's melody, my head swayed in serenity. *Born to be free* accompanied my thinking. *Oops! Look out ahead. Let's make room for that big guy on the road.* A logging transport approached in the opposite lane, fully loaded with massive logs.

Sheer volume and momentum created air suction when the big truck whooshed by only feet away. It was enough to rattle teeth and coffee cups inside the truck cab. Oh yes, a sensible time to hold the steering wheel with both hands, displaying white knuckles and focus ahead, steady-steady. The rhino-head trucker waved and tooted his horn in appreciation for yielding extra room on the road. From the size of the front grill, protected by iron bars and massive hooks for winching, there would be no arguments. He was much bigger. It was the law of the land.

Astor's white-knuckled grip on the steering wheel subsided. After making a fist close to his cheek, his elbow bent at ninety degrees as he pulled an imaginary cord hanging from the cab's ceiling. His lips rounded for blowing air out like a train whistle. The confined echo was an ear-deafening, vibrating noise performed by Astor to imitate a transport truck honking. To release some pressure at the stunt, my eyes bulged again. I shrugged it off, one hand prying my lower jaw down to pop the eardrums. And then we went rambling on. "I'm going fishing with my friends." I changed some of the lyrics. We bellowed out the song like two choir boys on Adderall. I couldn't help thinking, *we could get paid for this*.

Astor released one of his southern rebel cries, toothpick intact and all. We ate the road in front of us that day like there was no tomorrow. "Can't wait to be on the road again." Dirt and loose gravel were sprinkled across the paved road from constant heavy transport activity. From the passenger side mirror, clouds of dust rolled out behind the back tires and off where the wind blows into infinity. I plastered a smile on my face with enough exposed teeth for a toothpaste commercial.

Head up, I chuckled, mimicking a woodpecker on a tin roof. In my state of delirium, I slapped my knee, which somehow seemed to help hold my organs together. My head dropped between my knees while my fingertips gripped the sunbathed dashboard. I sat in a fetal position, rocking gently to soothe my gut. Amid laughter and fighting for breath, I managed to inform my traveling companion, "It hurts, please stop."

"Let's end it with one more *on the road again*," said Astor, "and one more rebel cry!"

After a short time, I finally straightened, and my thoughts gradually returned to sight-seeing. Although, periodically, my left foot kept tapping the mat, as I had trouble getting the song out of my head. "On the road again."

To the east, a congress of ravens soared high in a jet stream of blue sky. Dipping to one side with their long wedge tails, they crisscrossed each other in haphazard circles, except for one individual. He flew much lower than the group, to the point where I could see the outline of his large beak and relaxed legs dragging underneath his body. If I stood outside the vehicle, I'm sure I would have distinctly heard his monotone, croaking call. The low-pitched vocal cords of the ravens appeared to bounce off tombstones. Somehow, the hearts of the living knew that below, on the ground somewhere, an animal had died. Having the unusual omnivorous diet, the black hooligans would no doubt pick the carcass clean to the bones in a few days. Nature's way of controlling outbreaks—when consuming dead animals, the ravens were immune to all infectious diseases.

Breakdown

Astor had to pull over, as steam poured out from beneath the hood. I could smell antifreeze—not a good sign. Astor made a crooked face and growled under his breath while elbowing to turn onto the shoulder of the road. Several things went through my mind: The long wait after calling a tow truck. Canceling our fishing trip. Either prospect felt heart-wrenching and I could not help but throw back my head, distraught.

The driver caught my despair. "No worries," announced Astor. "The water pump belt broke; I have had a spare one since I knew it was going. Lately, it squeals when I start the engine."

Wonderful. I took a deep breath, loads coming off my chest. Who carried a spare water pump belt with tools to change it? I smiled to myself. Locals in the Yukon like Astor were the answer. "Do you need help?" I offered, hopeful.

"No, no," came the low reply. "Walk around, Joseph, and stretch your legs; changing the belt won't take long."

The truck's hood opened wide with a creak; wrenches clamored in a bunch when hand-picked by Astor. I let him do his mechanic thing and walked around. The air was fresh outside and my heart leaped; we were back on track to go fishing again. I took advantage of our unscheduled stop on the side of the road to go for a leak. While whistling a tune to myself, "On the road again," I casually strolled into the brush farther up past the ditch.

A mountain creek babbled below. Curious, I meandered down for a better look. Who knew, I might see fish underwater. No fish to be seen; instead, my ears caught the moaning of a child. Impossible, I reasoned. I must be hearing things. At the far edge of the creek yards away, I noticed a round shape. A bundle of black and some yellow rolled around under thick underbrush. I jumped over the creek for a closer inspection. What was going on over there? Ah! So cute. An orphan bear cub had gotten tangled up with a yellow nylon rope, possibly tossed from the road. Frayed with knots, the nylon rope circled the tiny bear's neck, body, and legs. Poor thing, scrawny and all alone. I was almost certain the distraught creature was crying out in bear language, saying, "Help me! Help me."

Like a Good Samaritan, that's what I did. Kneeling on the ground, I grabbed the little fellow by the loose skin on his shoulders and held him between my legs. Not wanting to waste time, I hurried, cutting the rope with my pocketknife one tangled mess at a time. When I finished, I stood up, still holding the cub by his loose skin, and had another bright Idea. I would show off my new friend to Astor. "Come on, little guy," I said. "You look a bit scrawny; I can feed you some milk from my lunch."

After my first step towards the truck, the bear cub started bawling as if being beaten to death. I needed to hold his behind with my other hand, I reasoned, to ease the pulling of the skin around his neck.

About that time, a roar exploded yards behind me. Oh God! What had I been thinking? An orphan be damned. The mother bear was present. A nine-foot wall of black fur stood on her hind legs, ragging on me. I swear, the open jaws of that mother bear were large enough to hold a person's head like a lollipop. Rows of canine teeth dripped foam, huge and frightening. Oh! and so close; right there.

The distraught mother bear roared blue murder with her front paws spreading out like frying pans. The claws stuck out, ready to shred. Good thing I had relieved myself minutes before. I dropped the bear cub from the waist high. The little whiner fur bag shrieked in pain when he hit the dirt, rolling to one side. I didn't care, but Mother responded by roaring even louder.

I'm outta here! I jumped back over the creek, running all out to the truck. No. I flew over the creek, praying, *please get me out of this mess, Jesus; I will give more to the church.* Running, I felt the wind in my ears; my heart wanted to come out of my chest. The hood of the truck slammed shut.

Astor saw the commotion and yelled out at me as he

opened his door, "Get in the truck! Get in the truck!"

I prayed some more. *Jesus, give me the strength to get inside the truck in time.* The broken belt had gotten fixed just in time, except for Astor's emergency toolbox left on the ground. The front tires flattened that out as the truck spit crushed stone from the rear tires, mixed with the clammer of wrenches. I started to breathe again once my door was shut. I fastened my seatbelt in silence, not believing what had just happened. A migraine was coming on. I hadn't noticed back there during the disaster, but the cub had intercepted the mother bear and, for comfort, ran between her legs.

Near the creek, satisfied, mother and cub strolled back in the forest. *I need to apologize to Astor.* "Sorry, Astor, I owe you a new toolbox with a good set of wrenches."

Astor waved that off. "Don't worry about the hardware, Joseph. I purchased that old box with all the tools for ten bucks at a garage sale five years ago." He turned to me, frowning. "What in heaven's name were you thinking, though, stealing a bear cub under its mother's nose? Are you out of your mind, Joe?"

I felt like a greenhorn, a dummy, and apologized profusely. "Sorry, Astor, I didn't know. I looked around and didn't see other bears, so I thought the cub had lost his mother. I wasn't thinking at the time."

"Obviously," he replied. "You almost died out there. My rifle is locked behind the seat; it would've taken too long to get it out."

Not looking at him, I mumbled once more in a low

voice, "Sorry, Astor." We drove in silence for a while, me, still drenched with sweat, contemplating how precarious life could be. I wanted to forget the whole foolish experience and move forward to go fishing.

After a prolonged stretch on the road, eroded foothills flanking the road, I noticed white blotches on one of the steep slopes. How out of place they seemed —we weren't in the Arctic, and it was late in the season for snow to cling in shaded areas this time of year, even in high altitudes facing north. I lowered my head to rub my temples and blinked before looking again to confirm what I'd seen.

Hold on a minute, that can't be right, snow doesn't move. Remembering the binoculars hanging around my neck, I reached for them and raised the lenses to the side window. As the leather strap shifted behind my neck, my index finger made the necessary adjustments to sharpen my view, tricky given the movement of the truck. We were moving at a good pace; I needed to trace the momentum by constantly shifting sideways and doing it fast before the blotches disappeared from view. Oh, man! My jaw dropped. A herd of Dall sheep was grazing in them hills. I couldn't help but whisper under my breath, "Wow!"

Emotions rose from my chest up to my head. *Bear in mind, you're in the Yukon now, Joseph.* A land yet to be fully discovered. Where communities banded together in dark winters and help could be found at your neighbours' houses. Where agreements were still made with a handshake. And where, on Sunday mornings, the church people sang that the love of Jesus was the only substitute to overwhelm the bad and make it turn around. Where during meals around kitchen tables, grandparents' gold rush adventures were still fresh in people's minds. Where elders affirmed that the steady hand of a big game hunter—who'd likely had at least one near-death experience, maybe many—was more precious than gold.

As we traveled along on the road, I couldn't help but imagine what it would be like to be sitting at the kitchen table in one of those camps just listening to old hunting stories. It didn't take long; my mind drifted away with the warmth inside the truck, and I imagined.

With a haze of pipe smoke hanging above the woodstove, a story emerged at the evening hunting camp. By the time the one-gallon coffee pot steamed hot over cast iron, accounts would thicken. The wannabe speaker cocked a leathery face while resting his hat on the edge of the table. The hunt was over for the day. Back straight, he sat down with a plunk, elbows out. His shoulders were thick from years of physical labour. Still sniffling loudly from yesterday's cold and without embarrassment, he rubbed the side of his nose with an open hand. His abdomen protruded when leaning to rock gently on the back legs. The chair creaked, back and forth, back and forth. The grey-haired man played up the moment, eager to spiel an adventure. He drew more attention by dislodging mucus down his throat and then deliberately leaning sideways to aim at the floor.

The spittoon was never far from his left foot; otherwise, the camp owner would have none of it. A splashing sound was common; still, when sitting around the table, no one ever had the stomach to look inside the spittoon. Both arms flew up, spaced midway to demonstrate a grave encounter with nature. Head reared to one side, his chest rose and fell with the effort.

Eager listeners leaned closer, jaws hanging open, holding their breath. Another deliberate gesture from *le raconteur*; all fingers parted to display possible panic in three seconds. One knee-high hunting boot rested flat on the floor, the other rose slightly, loose and ready for stomping at the climax. The technique was used by skilled storytellers to shake the audience down to their boots. The account traveled far back, the words stretching to build the tension. The speaker pointed a finger towards a window, in the direction of the wilderness beyond the glass. The camp's cook stopped halfway across the kitchen and turned to listen; a dishcloth flung over one shoulder. The plate at hand would be circle-whipped many times; going to the bathroom would have to wait. Words from the speaker spilled out.

"His decisive action and steady aim had been the difference between living and dying. Once engaged to charge, there was no turning back. The sheer roar of the great beast was deafening. No doubt, a single warning huff could change where the wind blew. His breath was horrid, rotten meat. The legendary King Kong gorilla left claw marks when stepping on a flat stone; so does this beast.

"After tracking all day, the big game hunter and the beast finally met in a clearing. What's worse than an old grumpy grizzly, you ask? An old grumpy grizzly with an abscessed tooth, that is what. With his monstrous head low to the ground and swaying sideways, froth poured from agitated lips. The foam strung out and whipped to the ground at every turn." According to the old hunter, the old bear had several broken teeth, with an abscessed tooth that had ballooned to the size of a baseball. Constant excruciating pain. Being elusive, normal for the old miserable bear, had been long thrust aside. Throbbing pain encumbered with rage dominated the creature, fang to claw. If something was not done quickly, a human head would be decapitated.

From the hunter's perspective, he saw a freight train of flexing muscles enlarging, running flat out. A lantern swinging on tracks could stop a train but not this hairy beast. This beast on his hind legs rose to the height of a two-story house. Only, yes, only the cool aim of a skilled big game hunter could save his own life. *Le raconteur's* foot slammed down. *Boom!* Plates and cups rattled. Spectators around the table pulled back, exhaled, and whipped their foreheads with the backs of their hands. Visibly distraught, the cook walked briskly towards the washroom, fumbling with his belt buckle.

The truck rumbled along, and I rested my head against

the back of the seat and continued to daydream about hunting camp. I envisioned being invited to join the men at their table after a long hunt. On and on stories would spill, deep in the night, including one about the lone wolf in early spring after several days of mild weather.

"As I recall last year," one of the men said, "not far from Silver Creek, a German tourist witnessed the ghost-like creature jumping over a wide expanse of open water. The wolf did this with grace and ease. From a human perspective, the feat was unimaginable."

Yet another added to the legend of the wolf. He cleared his throat for attention while twisting a clump of whiskers, clearly pondering how to proceed. With a hand finding the edge of his seat, the old timer shifted to relieve the numbness in his left leg. The pipe came out, clutched in one cupped hand as he packed tobacco with a yellowish index finger. His beard was long and grey, and, when speaking, syllables roll like butter over thin lips with no show of teeth. With an arm stretched out, he jabbed the tip of his pipe towards the outside door, which set the scene for what Grandpa Dugas was about to declare. Like a stiff board on hinges, the wiry body pivoted frontward to converse in secret with his few trustworthy companions. The grey one spoke, it seemed, with his glass eye that never blinked.

"When hiking in these parts, there's no such thing as spotting a wolf in the wild," Monsieur Dugas said, clearing his throat. "It's the other way around. The wolf has spotted you long before. Now, for no reason except being curious, that wolf allows people the rare privilege to take pictures and observe. But don't you look away for more than two seconds," the old-timer warned with the tip of his pipe in the air, "or the wolf may disappear on you?" The grandfather then leaned back and with precision struck a wooden match on the stem of his pipe. Call it a quick flash from the past—the sudden sulfur flare created a candle-lit portrait reminiscent of the one depicting an old man by Rembrandt.

Acquaintances readily agreed that Grandfather Dugas was not a pleasant man to look at, although dependable throughout his forty years as a welder in the Yukon. For the employer, that was all that mattered.

Caribou

Still looking outside of the truck window in a fog, I let my imagination flow even further.

Yet another tale emerged around the table concerning a handful of caribou stranded on spring ice floating along in the river. After coming out of the washroom with his plate, the cook joined in by walking over to the table, arms flaring, eager to tell his own story.

"Danger was floating all around the caribou in the deep, dark water," explained the cook. "Tentative muzzles in peril were stretched high towards the far shore while fidgeting hooves side-stepped the borderline of their icy prison. With the mild disturbances from the animals' hooves, ice chipped away from the edge and fell into the abyss. Necks were stretched out like giraffes. If animals could talk, you'd hear them calling out to the shore, 'Come nearer, come nearer.' Alas! Still, it was not near enough. A heartfelt decision needed to be made. That fast-flowing current was dragging the caribous far away from home, and downriver only got wider and wider.

"One bold individual jumped at the chance anyway. He leaped high and hard; all four legs stiffened to meet troubled waters. No surprise, the terror-stricken animal sank deep under the icy water. Not good, as the caribou need to breathe, the same as people. Excruciating seconds passed before a head and shoulders sprang to the surface, the caribou frantically swimming towards shore. Pink nostrils flared, blasting frigid air mixed with ice pellets. Water streamed off the caribou's dense fur coat, the long, hollow hair helping with buoyancy. From instinct, the animal had one objective: swim for the shoreline as quickly as possible. Thick white slabs of ice, bashing, grating opponents, disintegrating some, with pulverizing power churning and scraping against each other. The apocalyptic thunder, the roar infiltrated with froth—it was hell on earth.

"In a split second, one large chunk rolled over the exhausted caribou. Down under the animal sank again, this time, it seemed, forever." The cook pounded his palms on the table to emphasize his point. "A frantic crowd had gathered along the rushing shoreline. A mother standing next to me, children clinging to her, pressed both hands to her mouth and exclaimed, 'For the love of God, come back up!' For one then two minutes, nothing, zero. No more seasonal migration for our yearling caribou, no more skipping jubilant along stony soil, sand, and moss with the million other hooves that had followed that ancient path leading to grasslands. No more feasting on willow leaves choking low-land creeks, sedges, flowering tundra plants, and lichens.

"Even now, a pack of hungry wolves would be a welcome prospect, the odds of surviving facing them better than facing the churning water. But no, mercy me, heaven answered. Finally, the head miraculously reappeared above the water, now closer to shore. The floating ice was not as heavy, not as turbulent, at the edge of the river. Breaking through, the young caribou found concrete footing under the water; a rainbow appeared in the background, bridging the river. The submerged body rose from the deep into the shallow.

"We watchers could practically hear a symphony of angels singing in G minor. Our four-legged David had conquered the Goliath of water and ice and now stood on the shore with golden rays glowing on his back. First, the caribou's head lowered, and his body shook inches from side to side; then, the head followed, releasing buckets of ice water, a blast of white spray. The fine, crinkly under-fur with thick, hollowed hair had preserved the caribou's body heat and saved his life. A boisterous snort greeted those of us on shore, who responded with raised hands, clapping and shouting, 'Thank you, Jesus!'

"Tracing the cool air in an arc with his rubbery nose, the victorious, four-legged specimen immediately picked up the scent of his family, a traveling herd of caribou. Why stand around and wait? The one that hesitates may not have a second chance. One leap forward, two leaps sideways, with his hind legs lashing at the blue sky, our shaky-wet caribou shot out of sight in a burst of energy. The young buck took off kicking his feet towards the mighty river as if mocking it with his 'see you next year, chum' attitude."

I came back to the truck cab from storytelling. Farther along the road, as I was sight-seeing through a squished-bug-covered windshield, an elongated body of water came into view on my side of the road. It was a wide part of the Salmon River running northwest to Alaska. Gliding effortlessly on the surface of the water, thin red and yellow lines shifted together in a bunch with dots in the center. As Astor drove along, whistling, my head swiveled to the side widow so I could investigate further.

While squinting over my shoulder, I scratched my ribs, thinking. I could see now—a posse of kayakers was on the move. Familiarities came to mind; I knew this area. Scrap memories from years passed have triggered my instinct to be cautious. If I remember correctly, not far ahead the river narrowed against the rock cliffs rising from both banks. When a person stood on the shore at the last bend in the river, he could see the channel covered in white caps cascading around protruding rocks. It roared and tumbled for half a mile in the mist, vegetation rooted along vertical walls.

Not surprisingly, it was a popular canoe and hiking area for summer and winter tourists. Locals knew it as their backyard. Like our Canada goose, people flocked north every spring for the ultimate experience, especially German tourists. I remember one important detail, a well-intended signpost on the shore that pointed out where to get off before the life-threatening rapids began. The letters were large for reading at a glance when paddling far out. *STOP- Portage #23*. After hiking the twenty-minute portage trail with a canoe on your shoulders, accompanied by the sound of rushing water, it was back to smooth sailing again.

Up ahead, the pristine body of water curved even closer to the road. I could see bodies in excellent form with torsos hunched over for equilibrium, dipping paddles effortlessly to one side and then the other. I couldn't help but wonder if the kayakers sang while paddling as the French voyageurs did during the fur trade across Canada. *"Alouette, gentille alouette?"* Probably … not so much. Still, thinking about it made me smile. The kayaker's leg, stomach, and thigh muscles collaborated to stay afloat and paddle, paddle. Bodies flexed with decisions made in fractional seconds for the experience, the thrill of gliding on water. They travelled like free spirits, savouring the "big waters of thunder," as the local first nation would say.

There. the kayakers arrived at portage #23. What? Not even a paddle-stroke pause to glance towards shore and see the warning sign? No, they all plowed toward the cascading corridor of thundering waters. In their minds, portaging was not an option. That kind of reasoning, gentlemen, kayakers can explain in detail over refreshments at the kayak club. New members were always welcome.

As I recalled, cold temperatures had turned merciful

that winter, with not too many potholes after the spring thaw. Even so, as we drove, those troublesome potholes seemed to line up with the vehicle's suspension, no matter what. We were moving along quickly, anxious to arrive at our fishing destination. The air outside was nothing less than pure. Astor said, "Keep an eye out for moose," which pulled me out of my kayakers-at-the-club trance. "They can spring out from nowhere." I did not bother looking that time, but the toothpick switched sides. Astor continued, "The flies drive them crazy this time of year, so they head for open clearings to find relief in the wind. Although, standing neck deep in water, feeding at the bottom, is the best tactic."

Musing, I nodded and stared out the front window on Astor's side. The tall pines grew crowded together, creating pitch-black skirted with underbrush. The wall of evergreen could certainly hide large animals for a good twenty yards, even the white fur coat of the jackrabbit. We passed a large tree leaning precariously at a sharp angle out past the forest line and over the ditch. I suspected that on some windy day soon, the tree would uproot over the road allowance, with the top snapping onto the unforgiving pavement. Truckers would trample the top of the tree flat before the Department of Highways could remove it. Evidence of pine-cone seedlings crushed and scattered by tires whooshing by was all over the road.

Who knows, the old, wise forest had discovered another way to spread its seeds for the next generation.

Close Call

Out of nowhere, without warning, a deafening sound shook my eardrums. Not to exaggerate, but it vibrated clearly out my eyeballs and sent shivers through my body. The boom loomed so dominating that I felt surrounded by its wave. In a split second, my heart panicked and started racing. Somewhere close, something was deadly wrong. Dread consumed my thinking as I swiftly looked behind me. My mind screamed: *Is a transport about to ram us in the rear?* If so, we needed to get out of the way fast. I glanced over my shoulder. All clear behind me, nothing? My neck cracked as I swung around to peer out the front. Oh, shoot! A bull moose! It was standing huge and broadside in the middle of the road.

'G' forces kicked in. My chest jammed forward, the seatbelt digging into my shoulder. My nose jolted disturbingly close to the dashboard. The truck was braking hard, slowing down, but not fast enough. I glanced at Astor, silently asking him what we should do. White knuckles squeezed the steering wheel as he laid on the horn with his other hand. His shoulders pressed against the back of the seat; his elbows were locked, and his face was like stone. I felt powerless. There was nothing I could do to help except stare at the moose. An enormous mass of fur accelerates towards our windshield with unprecedented velocity.

I had always assumed a 4x4 pickup truck was as big as a bull moose. I was wrong. 'G' forces were at hand again as we swerved right, right. The body mass of dark fur shifted to the front left of our truck. Clip! With screeching tires, Astor swerved left, back onto the road.

The smell of burning rubber that accompanied the squealing tires cleared, and my seat belt went limp. Astor and I gazed at each other in dead silence, not a word. Then we instinctively stared at the road ahead and back at the speedometer—80 kilometres an hour. Astor spoke first. "That was close, too close. 80. I'll drive at that speed for a while."

More silence. It troubled me, so I had to ask, "Do you think the moose got hurt?"

His reply was immediate. "Oof." While leaning back, exhaling, Astor appeared to think carefully before adding, "I felt a light vibration in my steering wheel when the moose scraped along my fender; I think I nicked his hind leg, but not by much. Moose are resilient animals."

After swerving back onto the road, I checked my rear-view mirror and saw the moose jumping into the ditch and disappearing into the forest. A heavy load lifted from my shoulders as I contemplated the reality of dying in a moose accident. Frantic, I rubbed my whole face with an open hand. How and why had that happened? I felt responsible. Minutes before, Astor had asked me to be on the lookout. I swear that moose appeared on the road like angels do. I shared my shortcomings with Astor. "Sorry, Astor, you asked me to keep an eye out for moose; how can anyone miss that? The moose practically took up the whole bloody road standing broadside. I thought for certain I'd spot them miles ahead."

Nodding in sympathy, Astor veered his head towards me. The toothpick moved, and this time I welcomed the action. "Have you ever encountered a bull moose running through a dense forest in the fall?" he asked.

I drew silent for a minute, contemplating the question, before replying, "No, never."

Astor pointed through the windshield towards the forest. "Well, first, the moose head draws back to form a wedge with his antlers like a *V*, creating a living plow. When sensing a threat by smell or hearing, he needs to run and establish distance quickly. Eventually, he stops, shifts sideways, and swivels his donkey ears, listening to detect if he has succeeded in leaving the danger far behind. When a bull moose runs full tilt through a forest, you'll hear the sharp, echoing sound of antlers whacking wood. If the tree is small and flexible enough, it will give way to the moose rack; if not, the moose head will jerk sideways and give way to the tree. From a distance, you'd think the moose was travelling along a clear-cut trail in the forest. Like fish in water, the dense forest does not limit fluent movement for a bull moose. If the ground is low and spongy, the hooves spread like snowshoes, and with the animal's momentum, the moose skips across swampy terrain like a jackrabbit. A mature bull moose easily patrols its territory in the summer. Nothing is too steep or too swampy or too dense."

After a brief pause, Astor spoke again, quieter this time as though talking to himself. "That moose was running a bit funny when entering the woods." He pulled back his head with a huff, nodded, and, yes, moved the toothpick. "He should be all right, though," he mumbled. "They're thick-skinned creatures with the bone density of a ram's head." The verdict stood as he rubbed his face with an open hand as if to erase any negativity. From Astor's perspective, the moose would get along just fine.

Slowly, our thoughts drifted back to our fishing trip. Astor cautioned, saying. "I'll take an extra fifteen minutes to get there; we'll be slowing down for the rest of the trip."

From my perspective, the slowing down idea brought profound relief. I was eager to re-enforce Astor's sensible decision. "Yes, excellent plan, Astor, let's do that; you can even take thirty minutes; that's also fine with me."

Out of the blue, Astor slapped his right hand on the side of the steering wheel with a loud *Ha!* smirk. His head shot back, and he laughed like crazy. But the facade went crumbling midterm, Astor's vocals trailing to a squeak. By some miracle, the famous toothpick was still held in the corner of his mouth. It defied the laws of gravity. We both knew that what had happened back there was no laughing matter. The lingering feverish forehead and sticky armpits reminded me in case I was tempted to forget. Astor and I had almost died. Still, like in wartime, poking fun before or after a battle calmed the nerves and made a person's fortitude steady

Enough talk about war and almost dying. After all, we were on a fishing trip. My attention returned to the vast, untamed waterways, the Salmon River. To the Indigenous people, the river of life flowing northwest from the mountainous forest to the tundra met up with the Yukon River. The Alaskan territory came into play after, then down to the Bering Sea. With the natives' fabricated moose-skin canoes, exploring one tiny section of the river must have taken a season. Travelling the entire length would take a lifetime if it could be done. The Salmon River had nursed coastal species such as Salmon, Rainbow, Cutthroat trout, Artic-Char, Steelhead and many more that had spawned annually for millenniums. Furthermore, the legendary Salmon River sustained carnivores like the grizzly, brown and black bear, wolves and fox, to name the most prominent; also, the majestic eagle. People of the First Nations depended on the bountiful Salmon River for their livelihood.

Before the white man discovered the Yukon, if I

were an eagle flying high along the river, I would probably encounter a scenery like this: Fishing camps carved out of the forest would be spotted along the sandy shore miles ahead. Their fish-drying poles, fastened head high, were covered with pink flesh. In the mix, smoke streams bent horizontally idle in the clear sky. The aroma would force numerous raptors to dip a wing, circle high above, and lament, "A taste, a morsel if you please."

Rest assured, all birds flying high had witnessed countless busybodies on shore with canoes paddling in and out, hauling fish among youngsters chasing each other for fun and laughing. Adults with a mission to accomplish plenty would shout to direct loafers. Bursts of hooting and laughter would reverberate all around. I could guess some of their conversations. "Where's Mountain-bear getting all the big ones," one asked. Would Mountain-bear disclose his secret fishing hole?

"Over my dead body," was his reply.

Life was pleasant near the river—a nice breeze, no flies, and plenty to eat. Even at the end of the salmon-spawning life cycle, the rotting flesh fertilized numerous plant species along the riverbank—a well-established step in the ecosystem. The mute fish offered his own life so plants could thrive abundantly in the new year—a concept above all others. The results of that noble deed triumphed abundantly. By June, lush greenery would adorn the river's shoreline in a festive mood. Vibrant colors exploded in all directions, for our pleasure, it seemed. The aroma, the scenery, was breath-taking. For the thousands of people hiking along the river year after year, thanksgiving would rouse their souls to ponder, *who in heaven's name formulated such a plan?*

Driving uphill on an elevated stretch of the road, we encounter the Salmon River bending its way to the sea. In a breath, the land rose to white-capped mountains—Dall sheep and wild goat territory. Like a snake in long grass, the river curved, peaceful in her elements. With eagles soaring above, heaven couldn't be far. Sometimes people forgot what time and nature could achieve; like an hourglass, erosion constantly trickled along the river's flank. The shifting water carried sediment, sand, and pebbles farther down to the next bend, eventually, with time, creating a meander. In doing so, the river will ultimately meet and break through and start a never-ending cycle. The result is a horseshoe-shaped Oxbow Lake remnant. Cut off from the river flow, the Oxbow Lake turned to marshland or dried up entirely. A person could walk in the middle of the ancient Oxbow Lake formation without knowing. Even sea turtles have not yet witnessed a full geological term; it takes hundreds and hundreds of years for a river to form an Oxbow Lake.

As we continued driving downhill, the Salmon River bows aside, leaving an expanse of lowlands crowding the highway. Grey tree trunks embedded in black muck brought to mind gigantic spears thrust from above by some ancient battle. Long void of leaves, several of them were pierced in the lanky poles, sought-after havens by woodpeckers and owls for nesting.

Vigorous in form, twisting vines consoled the once thriving heavyweight by spiralling up the trunk, displaying green leaves with red undersides. The colourful plants attached themselves to the bark with needle precision. The goal was to bask in the sun, flower purple-red, and brighten the day.

Near the road, pool-sized bodies of open water interconnected with chocolate-coloured channels lie dormant. In contrast with the forest green stood dark brown muskrat lodges; they appeared beaten like last year's haystacks. A colony of flat tails thrived in those waters. The muskrat lodge was a brilliant way to prevent being eaten by intruders. The entrance and exit can only be accessed underwater, somehow calculated by instinct below the freezing depth of winter ice. Inside, the tunnel curled up swiftly to the centre core above the water line from the outside. This created a high and dry dome living area, all below-freezing temperatures in winter. The industrious muskrats could chomp on fresh roots at their leisure and raise litters of five to six kits in relative safety twice a year. They slept huddled together as a family and grew fast, learning from each other how to survive in the muskrat world. To some degree, the whole lodge structure floated and rose and fell with spring floods and summer droughts. Logs floating nearby were smeared with fresh mud and used as diving platforms to get away. The mowing of cattails and green grass floating nearby along open water was evidence of a healthy community. They consumed much vegetation without scruples, leaving fresh piles of oval pellets behind.

The sight, as we drove by, was priceless. I thought *pearls do thrive on country ponds*. With a golden centre guarded by pure white petals, the lily flower hovered just above the water as if by magic. Their rounded pads formed green carpets that spread over the tranquil water. Amphibians rested on top to croak for a mate or to poke their heads between the leaves for optimal camouflage. White lilies are one of the oldest aquatic plants—a symbol of purity and chastity. Reminiscent of miniature white roses on wedding cakes, I wanted to sneak over there and eat one. Nearby, the rigid stalk of arrowheads stood defiant against the north wind to show its blooming flower.

Feeding in seconds, the hummingbird danced mid-air while immersed headlong in the colourful flower. Red-currant berries hung in clumps over the still water at the far side of one pool, casting intricate shadows that swayed in the breeze. Sheltered from predators above, schools of minnows toured hourly, waiting for the red-currant manna to drop from the sky.

Like granite on two steel rods, the blue heron would not fidget. It stood superior, high-legged, with folded neck pressed to her blue body. The calm waterways were teaming with life. Unlike the doctor's office, the blue heron didn't have to wait long. If I hadn't been inside the truck, I would have heard a distinctive plunging splash and witnessed breakfast being swallowed whole. Not a good day to be a catfish.

A flock of red-winged blackbirds brushing tips in a dark, turbulent cloud descended low in a woosh, then cut high back to right-low, only to spread apart in a whirlwind on a field of cattails. Perched slanting and screeching, elaborate heads bobbing, the fiery birds swayed in the wind while holding on to the plants. Poof! On a whim, the multitude resumed flight in tight formation without knowing where to settle next. The area was immense and spread for miles around. The sun-bathed flatlands delivered bonanza vegetation, which offered unique fruits and seedlings for countless species. The result was a constant exhibition of day-to-day living on the move.

We lightened our speed for the sharp curve in the road ahead. Without fanfare, the scenery changed altogether. Land and the acute crown of trees continued to the blue sky. On the opposite riverbank, bald eagles were perched midway up a stretch of towering timber. With their heads to one side, the raptors' one eye diligently scanned the river's surface for swimming shadows. I noticed a flight movement from the corner of my eye. An eagle took the plunge from his lookout, sweeping down with incredible lightning speed. Cutting a white line along the river's surface, readied talons dragging. Whoosh! Under the eagle's body of wind-blown feathers, the split-second white-water disturbance delivered results. A sizable fish in mid-air disappeared once, twice, three times under the labouring wings, dripping heavily. The stringy neck plumage of the eagle flexed and bowed under the strain of rising. From an instinctive reflex to dislodge itself, the frantic fish whipped its tail left, right, left, right, in protest. Two juveniles were waiting at the cliff in the eagle's nest. What a spectacle that was. Astor witnessed the eagle snatching the fish from the water's surface and asked, to no one in particular, "Who said that fish can't fly over treetops?"

Only in the Yukon, they say.

Stuck in the Mud

We got stuck in the mud. When stuck with a 4x4 pick-up, there's no such thing as getting out and pushing. We needed a winch or another 4x4 truck to pull us out. Our pick-up truck was sunk big time, almost to the axle. The flat-tailed creatures were the culprits responsible for us being stranded. An industrious beaver family had dammed the stream crossing beneath the road. As a result, water had backed up over the road three feet deep and a hundred feet wide. Now we were comatose in the middle of it all, going nowhere.

This time, though, providence was on our side. A six-wheeler Argo came drudging along from behind and around our truck as if appearing from nowhere. As Astor stuck his head out the window, words were exchanged with the two robust occupants sitting in the six-wheeler. Great! They drove up on dry land and then stretched a steel cable attached to our truck's front hook specially designed for winching. With the truck's transmission in neutral, we creaked forward, and after ten yards or so, we finally got out of the mud and onto solid ground. I stayed in the truck, relieved, smiling ear to ear, and grateful. Astor got out and, with a handshake, thanked the two good Samaritans for pulling us out. As Astor walked back to the truck dripping in mud, more hand waving was exchanged along with the encouragement to "Have a safe fishing trip," that was it. No fuss, not complicated.

Finally, we slowed down to make a right on a gravel road for the last half hour of the drive. Not long after the dust settled, we rolled to a crunchy halt on crushed stone. Our time of being in air conditioning without mosquitos was over. After stepping outside, I could hear the engine ping and the smell of heated motor oil mixed with antifreeze. I still had my hand on the truck's handle when I turned to face a wall of solid granite six feet away, blocking my view—a natural monument covered with pale mushrooms, green moss, and oozing moisture. Roots invaded the six-foot façade in and along every visible crevice. The rock cut jutted out on either side for short distances at human height both ways before curving downward and disappearing to normal ground level.

A recently broken tree top lay in the middle of the trail, still green and loaded with gummy pinecones. Studying it, I understood what had taken place. A century-old jack pine had attempted to grow in shallow soil over bedrock, and something, likely a thunderstorm, had uprooted it. The jack pine had fallen over a trunk-sized boulder and gotten hung up. The top must have broken off and tumbled on our path at the sudden jolt. With half the roots still attached to the soil, the straight log cabin beam carried on, pointing toward the sky at a thirty-degree angle. High and dry, it would remain stationary for years to come.

Fresh pinecones, likely knocked loose from the top end of the tree, were strewn in a pile below. For squirrels, it would be an excellent strategic point to sit, watch out for predators, and, like pros, tear apart pinecones for their seeds. Heavy tree limbs angling just above the tip of the pole would do for plan "B" for the squirrel's speedy getaway if needed.

If a pine marten attempted to engage its fidgeting but alert prey sitting at the end, the chase would end poorly for the marten. Beyond the rock cut by the road, the ground was flat, rising gently northeast. I took a few more steps and lowered my head to contemplate my laced boots. My mind idled while shifting gravel with my boot for no practical reason. I had a troubling itch, a question for Astor, and came out with it.

"Where did you say the wolves were howling last night, Astor?"

Astor's body seemed to be in pain when he stretched. He rubbed the back of his neck as if he had a severe headache. He lifted his chin to gaze into the distance. His calloused hands closed into fists and rested on both hips as he stood, legs apart. With his lips gradually shaping for words, I could sense a man gathering information while conscious of how it would affect the outcome. That was when the toothpick moved to the other side. At the time, I reasoned that tipping back the Australian hat made the question appear much more complex.

"Yes, I heard them all right," said Astor. "The howling originated far out there; there's no debate. But south, yes south, on the other side of the river."

That was it. That was his answer at the time. If you asked me, it was barely worth it for the toothpick to have switched sides. Oh, that one was new? When my back was turned for a minute, I heard a loud lip smack before Astor announced, "We better get moving, Joe. We have three hours of fishing and one for walking to our fishing area and back to the truck."

The back of the truck opened with a well-designed click. While flexing a knee, I applied pressure on my foot. Pressing the edge of the tailgate and utilizing my other leg for momentum, I hauled myself into the box. Youthfulness was on my side. I straightened, legs apart, and surveyed the fishing equipment. Hop climbing into the back of a 4x4 was not one of Astor's best moves. He usually resigned himself respectfully and let me have a go.

Astor's fishing gear was packed in a wood box laminated on the inside with inch-thick foam for bumpy roads. It wasn't pretty, but it did the job. The old, beat-up metal cooler strapped with bungee cords next to it was a match made in heaven. Astor proudly told me on most fishing trips, "The cooler is large enough to handle four twenty-pound fish; anything more, we use our fillet knife, start cutting heads, and have a fish fry at the shore."

Astor is not a fan of stuffing trophies to hang on a wall in a man cave; that's a waste of money, as far as he's concerned. In all activities performed, the wise grey owl loves to lecture on how things need to get done. The instructions came out direct: "Preparation and set-up are everything." When one of Astor's lectures emerged, I habitually turned around, cleared my throat, and rolled my eyes, not necessarily in that order.

When we headed out, my insides craved getting on with the fishing business. Like a soldier in training, I was glad to conquer the early morning rise. My efforts would be rewarded if I could reel in a monster. We had packed a small ice cooler in one backpack to store the fish in. That should hold them until we got back and transferred our catch to the main cooler in the truck. "Don't forget, Joe; we keep the fish cool until you eat or freeze them" This was another of Astor's "on the fly" fishing trip quotations. An explanation always followed serene instructions. Astor would never stray from his fishing guide mindset until death did us part. That also included the undisputed toothpick.

I usually responded with a hand wave as I walked away from him. "Yes, yes, Astor. I get it, and that too." And yes, I'd clear my throat and roll my eyes.

I had not noticed when immersed in preparation, but the morning fog gradually lifted around us. Astor and I stood with thumbs under our shoulder straps; our upper bodies jerked upward to help align the weight on our backs. Foreseeing thick underbrush and bugs in our immediate travels, we firmly lowered our caps until they grazed our ears. All smirks, we turned, eyeing each other. Monsieur fishing guide pointed his gnarled finger in the general direction he wanted us to go. And then we were off, army boots snapping dry twigs, fishing rods in hand, and ready to roll. Astor called out to the whole forest like a booming sergeant while leading, "Now, let's not waste that ice, shall we?"

In the early travels of that fateful walk on the trail, my past gradually dissipated in my consciousness; my mind went peaceful. The forest coaxed us to press on like the gentle breeze on our cheeks. With every step, my senses aligned themselves with the nature sprouting around me. I swear my eyes could virtually peer through the tree trunks at specific points during the walk, knowing what lay behind them. I felt like a true mountain man survivor. Leg muscles had shifted to facilitate walking downhill.

Above us, frisky birds made short appearances on branches as we walked. Performing head flicks, staring down at us, lop-sided, they twittered, *chick-a-dee-dee-dee*, repeat, repeat, and then ruffled their feathers as though in disbelief before taking off without a backwards glance. The tiny birds' behaviour reminded me of what mother used to say, "Some people don't know how to visit; they walk inside the house like a fence post and then sit with one cheek on the corner of their chair, announcing, "We need to leave soon." To add insult to injury, they take one sip from Mama's fine bone china teacup and then depart. What was up with that? You might as well stay home. Yes, Mother.

Whole tree logs with roots attached were scattered among wind-swept shrubs that had sprung up since the last flood. These forced us to deviate from the beaten path, raised elbows protecting our eyes from thickets whipping back. I smelled fish in the air, confirmed by the cries of eagles.

When we finally broke through over high terrain, a large expanse came to view the Salmon River. Out of sight, beyond savage, the mighty river migrated relentlessly towards the Bering Sea. Sparkling turquoise shifted, displaying a fast flow. The white-water shoreline over polished rock made entry questionable. A distant rumbling spelled out the warning, "This is no place to swim."

On the south side of the river, hundreds of stones from knee-high to truck-sized littered the sandy shoreline as far as we could see, curving northward behind rising land. The spectacle gave the impression that, at one point, giants had played with marbles and left in a hurry.

After walking in silence for a while, we came across thousands of diamond-shaped imprints along the shoreline. From a distance, I thought natives had spread out fish nets on the sand. Stepping closer, I noticed hundreds of bits of shells and footprints. Shorebirds had been walking constantly in and out of the water from the open, sandy beach. A gemstone site for birds to feed, rest, and receive warning of predators. I heard the cry and lifted my head. High above, an eagle circled tenaciously as if one leg was tied to the bottom of the river. With its telescopic eyes, the opportunity to spot a meal soon came. Bombs away, free fall was at hand, the distance between them closed by the pursuer. The prey quickly vanished. This outcome would surprise many. Sometimes eagles do look scraggy for a good reason.

We were getting close to our fishing site. At one point, I found myself alone on the bank of the Salmon River, peering across to the other side. I still remember the mid-day hour standing on high ground, breathing in the spectacular. I didn't notice for a while, but a short way back, Astor's footsteps had trailed behind and branched away from me. The offshoot beaten path soon took him to a clearing.

Once he arrived to a dead end, the wind quieted down with the river's roar more distant. A crystal-clear pond an acre in size, lay in the centre of the clearing. Tall weeds toed around the drop-off zone below, with plenty mowed close to the roots under the water. The beaver grass floated like straw, with milky white stems to pointed green tips. The muskrat's clan was busy harvesting that week. New and old webbed footprints in pliable mud covered the bank. Making a nuisance of himself, the opportunistic fox left his mud tracks zigzagging aimlessly to sniff out prey. From Astor's perspective, the area predisposed a tapestry of everyday living in the wild except for another footprint that left him standing, scratching his head and frowning.

Back at the house, I close my eyes and rub my face

with both hands to come out of my storytelling for a minute. Lillian is asleep on the couch. I glance sideways at the clock to see if Finn and Diane are still attentive. They are. I point to the floor and blurt out, "The wolves were much closer than we'd anticipated."

With that, I resume my story.

"I can tell you this with certainty: after all these years, I still recall the hour, the first time I felt a sense of uneasiness crawling on my back. The sort that makes you spin around to look, just in case. It surprised me to find myself walking alone but I was not overly concerned; Astor did that sometimes, walking out of range without a word. Stopping to lean against a tree and rest, I broke bits of twigs with my thumbs and tossed them around while scanning the surroundings for my guide to show up. It didn't take long; beyond the tree trunks across a meadow, my eyes fell on a man walking briskly towards me.

"What were you looking at down there, Astor?"

He waved me off impatiently and said, "Wolf tracks."

Surprised, I stood there and waited until he got close before asking, "What wolf tracks?"

"Didn't you see them? The tracks crossed our path a short while ago."

"Nope, sorry, didn't see a thing."

Astor sighed deeply. "Sometimes, Joe, when spotting fresh animal tracks, you can be as blind as a housefly on a windowpane." After a sniff, he cleared his throat and spat on the ground behind him. Astor explained to me what he'd seen when crouching back there. Oddly enough, the toothpick didn't move. "At that pond, we passed, I came across a fist size impression an inch deep in soft clay. The broad wolf track overlapped all others in the mud. The edges hadn't collapsed yet, so they were recent, maybe early this morning, heading for the woods. The evidence showed one mature animal, but don't be fooled by the one animal theory, Joe; the odds are that the lone ranger is not so alone. The leader is probably an experienced female crossing in and out on the riverbed to flush out any large prey.

I frowned. "Are you sure about the last part, Astor?"

He didn't hesitate to answer, "Yes. In hunting season, we call that *dogging*, and you can rest assured that the wolf's partners in crime are waiting ahead and out of sight, fully rested, ready to sprint in a flanking position for an ambush. They are well organized, hunt in packs, and are efficient. In late fall, they do the opposite. Packs of wolves will drive large prey towards the river onto thin ice. You know the outcome." He lowered his voice and turned reflective. "Still, hunting in the middle of the day is unusual; they must be hungry."

I didn't want to hear that when we were close to our fishing spot. Astor was an experienced woodsman, so I gave him a choice. "Do we continue or go back? It's up to you; you're the guide on this fishing trip."

"No, we continue." Saying that he swung his backpack in front of him and reached into one of the deep side pockets. I found myself staring at a .45 Magnum revolver pointed at the sky. Astor was grinning ear to ear. Surprised, I did not even see the toothpick flinching. "You fire a couple of shots in the air with this baby, Joe, and we won't have to worry about wolves getting too close.

I also grinned ear to ear and said, "Astor, you're a genius."

He returned the weapon to his pack. "I've been waiting too long for this important fishing trip to be postponed because of wolves."

I nodded. "So, we split up here?"

"Yep. You see any wolves, holler."

I started for my fishing spot, Astor walking along the river in the opposite direction. As I trotted along, I reflected on my friendship with my guide. I had heard him tell people how we met so often that I knew it by heart, and it flooded my mind now.

We'd been introduced by a co-worker three years before at a Christmas social event. The gathering consisted of provincial government employees working alongside people with special needs and recovering addicts from all walks of life. Qualifications for the program required being mechanically inclined and enjoying working with wood. Even if you weren't mechanical, anyone could fetch boards, hand over wood screws, and clean up shop if their hearts were in the right place. Astor, a long-time volunteer and favourable customer, personally grew into the family team. An older brother ten years his senior was also part of the team; his name was *P'ti-Gas*; in short, little guy. French irony, as the man was over six feet tall with 250 pounds of muscle attached to bear paws that hung below the knees. The team learned quickly to stand rigid, fill their lungs, and protect their ribs when *P'ti-Gas* walked by.

The bearded brute would sneak behind to give anyone a bear hug, leaving their feet dangling. Why? Because *P'ti-Gas* was happy to see them, and yes, he wanted to. Hold on to your rib cage, people! Punch the his hairy arms if it makes you feel better, but no arguments, just a plea. "Okay, that's enough now, *P'ti-Gas; Joseph* can't breathe. Down now. Down. Down." A gentle giant who didn't know his strength. He even was less delicate when working with the shop tools. If the job didn't go *P'ti-Gas's* way, the woodworking tool would be bent, broken, or tossed in the corner. Hey, it was the nature of the beast. After ten wonderful years in the shop program, it ended one day when *P'ti-Gas* died peacefully in his sleep at Auntie Jane's home—enlarged heart failure, the doctor said, which didn't surprise anyone. Although the re-tooling budget for the shop improved, the church service was packed; everyone loved *P'ti-Gas*.

The eight-thousand-square-foot wood shop had wall-to-wall conduits connected to a roaring dust collector on the roof's kiosk and was well equipped with German-engineered, cast-iron woodworking machinery built in the 50s. The equipment weighed a ton and lasted forever. Like a modular assembly line in progress, the dedicated working team built doghouses, more doghouses, park benches, stools, and picnic tables of practical styles and sizes in solid pine or, sometimes, for indoor use, white birch. No sawdust wood boards were allowed; that would be an affront to the authentic, wood-working connoisseurs.

Tracie was the most gifted cabinet finisher in the class; she could calculate complex angle cutting for the table saw with pencil line precision like no other. A massive billboard outside facing the well-travelled Caribou Street said it all: "Open to the public." Local provincial and city parks were serious big-order customers who purchased countless benches and picnic tables. Pine boards treated with water-repellent stain and natural white cedar were used to face the elements for future generations. The proceeds from sales kept the facility solvent with wages, utilities, field trips, and the Christmas get-together. It was *P'ti-Gas's* job to cut down the Christmas tree, and for ten years *he had* dragged his gigantic tree that was too big and too high into the hallway. The staff members scratched their heads, wondering where to put that monstrous tree.

Years have passed since the death of his older brother and three years since Astor had first shaken hands with a young man named Joseph from the southern city. In a festive crowd, an introvert like Astor preferred to sit back and listen. As for me, the man of the hour, it was the complete opposite; my life was an open book for all to pick at. I'd spark a topic at the tip of a hat with any warm body willing to converse. That evening, the spiked cranberry fruit punch dislodged tongues, and conversations piled high with goals, bucket lists, and adventure stories. Yep, I, the stage performer, applied hand gestures, emphasizing ingenious planning; after all, I did have French blood in me.

According to an old topography map, I could explain what area I wanted to explore. The map charted a steep ravine with an abandoned gold mine waiting to be rediscovered. "The technology for detecting gold nuggets has improved since the turn of the century." I, the self-taught geologist, gestured with open hands as though this were common knowledge. I felt confident that I, Joseph, could face the challenges of nature with sheer determination. "All you needed," I concluded, "was a docile packing mule, a prospector tent, water, a rifle, a metal detector, and music." After all, I'd grown up watching old Western movies where cowboys bedded under the stars using a log as a pillow with no bugs and no rain if you picked the right time. My philosophy was to do it and figure things out along the way.

I'd paused for an icy cranberry sip, wide-eyed with lifted eyebrows, ready to defend my position. No one bothered arguing. Some rolled their eyes; others walked away. Astor told me later he'd listened, alarmed, thinking to himself, *what world does this city boy Joseph live in? By the end of the year, that young buck will be a circle on a rescue map with everyone searching for him.*

Having my kind of attitude up north in the Yukon is a sure recipe for disasters, like losing toes due to frostbite or worse. Speaking with so much confidence and few resources to fall back on was absurd for an experienced fishing guide like Astor. But I shrugged off all negativity from others who advised restraint; my enthusiasm was unrivalled. My profession as a teacher for people with special needs moved Astor more than my enthusiasm; however, since his older brother, *P'ti-Gas,* had been involved in the program for many years, like blood brothers, old Astor and your father had an ingrained passion for enriching the lives of the less fortunate. To make a difference no matter how monotonous or trivial it seemed.

On that very evening, the invitation Astor offered was heartfelt. "Let's go fishing sometime, Joe." The rest is history.

The packed trail turned on itself, zigzagging down to the river a hundred feet below. I started jogging until I stood at my first, long-awaited fishing spot. As I shifted my body to loosen my load, both hands slid under the straps of my backpack. I then pressed forward, letting my forearms scrape under. Gravity accomplished the rest. The cumbersome pack flopped in a tinkling clamour of tin cups and utensils.

I lowered my gaze briefly to direct my boot, packing a flat surface among mismatched pebbles. Then I knelt on the ground, facing the pack. Grunt. "Who did that double knot?" I mumbled to myself. Hurried fingers fumbled with the braided cord securing the opening. The stainless-steel coffee thermos flew out, arcing to land on the flattened gravel. I jammed a hand inside my front left pocket and grabbed my sunglasses, unfolding them with a flick of the wrist. Shifting surface glare would not encumber this stylish angler, *moi*.

My fishing rod was jammed between my legs just above the knee. Why put it on the ground, people? That would result in losing valuable fishing time.

Where was Astor at the time? Not my concern. Probably fishing over the other end of the cliff, I thought at the time.

Ready for anything and standing on tiptoes, *moi*, the eager fisherman, scanned the surface for deep water holes, spotting two possibilities. With my arm stretched way back, I swung and released. The fishing line arced over the dark area before splashing into the water felt sweet. The well-greased gears inside the reel purred like a cat. I reeled in methodically, jiggling occasionally, attentive to setting the fishhook in a flash. The ten-pound fishing line had been recently replaced, the drag checked and fine-tuned like a pro. Lures and fish bait used at the time cannot be divulged, as they are sacred.

Skies were cloudy, with no shadows to be seen. One final sunglass adjustment just because. *Hold on, is this possible?* Joe, the man, could smell a big one lurking. *Come on, big fish, come to Uncle Joe.* Purrrr-purrrr.

Wolves

Wolves—a pack seven strong—approached along the river on our side. I was preoccupied with fishing until I spotted movements while casting. Wolves, what to do? Quickly, I decided to leave my gear on shore to investigate and find Astor. With the rod resting over a log, I wedged my handle into the stony shoreline and began climbing back to the steep riverbank path for a better look.

Once on top, I ran in a stooped posture behind some trees, alert to any movement around me. I hid there to spy on the wolves' approach, deliberating what to do next. I looked around and behind me. Should I find Astor with the gun first or yell "Wolves!" to see if he showed up?

At that moment, in a heartbeat, the wolf pack's direction changed drastically, and curiosity got the best of me; I decided to wait and see why they had switched courses so abruptly away from the river. If they turned towards our fishing site, I promised to alert Astor. At the time, I wouldn't say I liked cancelling fishing or firing a gun. From my hideout, I raised the binoculars hanging around my neck to my eyes, both hands trembling.

They carried themselves with ease, those wolves, tall from the shoulders and with long bodies. Their bushy tails swayed in the wind. Far above the ridge and with my handy binoculars, I could easily detect the wolves' rib cages sticking out. They were starving. Whom are they going after, and where? I could imagine that burrows of small mammals in the wolf's path were fearful beyond measure. For the weary mouse, detouring around large rocks inside elaborate tunnels called home would pay off. Woody, the mouse, must be hiding deep underground without a squeak. Dreaded canine footsteps above ground are getting closer and closing in. For the pack, when the opportunity presented itself, they would snatch a morsel along the way, so why the fuss?

Being early summer, the thick winter fur of the wolves was in the final shedding mode. Now spent and obsolete for preserving body heat, it hung in clumps of matted hair, flopping with every stride. As the British would say, "Their coats were in a bloody mess." Close to pan-size paws spread to accommodate deep snow, although they were now pressed flat on hard gravel. The rounded claws on lanky legs appeared awkward and out of touch for the summer months, presenting zero comforts for shoulder joints. Muscle pain had to be constant.

Their wide-open throats assisted with excess airflow when running as a pack, thus ventilating over heated bodies. The result forced their upper lip to flap in the breeze when on the move, displaying ivory teeth biting the wind at every stride as if needing the practice how to eat.

I focused on the worst specimen in need with my binoculars—an alpha female likely nursing pups. She had washboard ribs with a stomach glued to her spine. The milk flow for her puppies had undoubtedly been reduced to pitiful drops. The wolves paused to look around. Were their hunger pains intensifying? Starvation was likely proving to be a loyal companion lurking inside the bone marrow, creating irrational behaviour.

To make matters worse, what looked to be a recent infestation of mange caused by mites wouldn't help much. For a last effort as a pack, the wolves were clearly shoving all that aside. The natural-born instinct to survive would narrow the view to one objective: act boldly, attack, and obtain food without considering possible injuries or death. For the pack of seven wolves, hunger demanded a breakthrough this very hour, or the puppies would die.

Had the eye of the cunning alpha male caught a glimpse of a tall figure with arms outstretched at the river's edge—me? Up on the ridge, I attempted to hide from his keen gaze under a bushy pine tree, but I was likely much too clumsy and slow. In the wolf's mind, chasing after a creature with only two legs would be like skipping over to Grandma's house.

Thank God! Heaven intervened. At that precise

moment, a familiar odour drifted across from the southwest. The wolves had to lower their heads to shelter their sensitive noses from the strong smell. With flaring nostrils at total capacity for scent, the sinus cavities were coaxed to flush out the compelling odour with gasping and sneezing. In a bizarre ritual, the wolves' heads shook downward, front paws scrubbing their long snouts in a fruitless attempt to shut the air passages. Irritated, they repeatedly shook their heads and sneezed and sneezed.

The smell was legendary, so sweet, so overpowering. From sheer intoxication, the three zealous wolves in front halted before their mind could direct good judgment. The four-legged bozos from the rear did not fare better; they all tangled up over their front paws, colliding with the three stationary bodies. In an emergency response, the tipsy wolves jolted to one side in confusion. What? What!

The wolves sidestepped each other's clumsiness with growls and snarls. The alpha male wasted no time restoring order. He circled the confused bunch, head low with curled upper lip showing sharp rows of ivory teeth. His ears were folded back, the hair on his shoulders spiking. In a low, threatening posture, the seriously mean-spirited wolf nipped their ankles as a reminder: I'm the boss; quiet down, I say.

The band struggled to recover some dignity. Male egos were bruised; repercussion followed in growls and yelps. Hauling acute hunger like an anvil around their necks, the incident was soon forgotten. The odour lurked immense now. The alpha wolf spiralled to the top of the ridge for a better look. As I watched through the binoculars, the quick decision was made for all to fall in line. I could practically read the alpha male's mind. *Forget the scrawny one on two legs. Let's head for the moose; we're all better acquainted with the moose.*"

One by one, in a coordinated fashion, the wolves changed direction. There was work to be done. They lowered their heads, seven pairs of yellow eyes peering through tall grass. Data bursting into the animal's brain had to register crystal clear: a moose out in the open. Quite near, right over yonder, and there was blood. More than ever, it was crucial for the wolves to turn invisible and drift, silent like ducks on a pond.

Along with grayish-brown fur, clumps of underbrush shadowing swampy vegetation was welcome camouflage for an ambush. The alpha male led the way. The killing zone, picked in advance by instinct, was near the boulder. Strategies of a wolf pack would have been witnessed countless times by juveniles and orchestrated in hundreds of plots as adults. Three parted to the left, and four went right without fanfare, fanning out to establish a large semi-circle around the moose. Sheer exhaustion revealed itself in a pause to a stride, shoulders failing to cooperate. The alpha female stumbled over her front legs. Still, with headlong determination, she found the strength to recover as she had undoubtedly done countless times on her journey "for the pups."

Once again, precious energy evaporated, and the

precipice of starvation prowled nearer. For the pack of seven, the hour had come to crouch in the cool grass, rest, and consider. An ancient Roman siege was taking place before my eyes. With numbers on their side, encirclement made sense. Dig in and wait for an opportunity. Time and patience were all required to probe, detect an opening, and attack.

Meanwhile, the scent of fresh blood quadrupled in the air. How could they not lick their upper lips? It wouldn't be long now. In his darkest hour, the old, injured moose will be brought to his knees by the pack of hungry wolves. The moose's final, precious deed is at hand—spilling his blood to regenerate new life.

The pups would live.

The Angels

After Astor found me under the pine tree peering through my binoculars, he slapped my back before speaking. "Are you okay, Joe? I lowered the binoculars, turned, and gave him a blank look without speaking. He shot a look over his shoulders. "Stop observing the wolves; they're no threat to us; instead, look up over the treetops."

I did, and, oh my gosh! Two brilliant giant figures stood on top of the trees in mid-air. My God! Were these angels? Without looking at him, I asked, "You knew about this, Astor."

"Yes."

I had a hundred more questions but didn't know how to begin. Instead, I stood there, my mouth hanging wide open.

Astor lifted a wedge hand close to my face and then pointed at a dark mass below us, near the boulder. There stood the most gigantic bull moose I have ever seen. That was when I understood what he'd meant about the wolves being no threat to us—they were preoccupied with the moose.

He stepped back. "Go get your fishing rod and stuff and then come back and meet me. Don't worry about a thing, Joe; it's all working out according to our plan. I'll be down there, waiting to answer all your questions."

Whose plan? Did *this trip* have anything to do with the angels? Before I could ask, Astor took off, rubbing the back of his neck with no more explanation. My legs shook uncontrollably as I watched him go. I forced myself to pick my way carefully down to the river. After retrieving my rod and gear, I started in the direction of where Astor was waiting on the other side of the river. Questions whirled through my mind as I trudged toward him through all sorts of tangled underbrush. What is that old guy up to? Why and how did those two angels arrive here? Were they still visible? And, again, whose plan? And finally, am I going to die soon?

I received one answer right away by looking up. Oh! The apparition of the two angels was still in plain view for an entire city to witness as I reached a tall, grassy clearing. I couldn't help myself; I tipped my head to look up, lifted both hands in reverence, and stood there awed. Something like a rectangular, no, square window frame hung suspended in the blue sky. The structure was immersed in flames swirling around it but not consuming it. Smoke? No, too silvery for smoke. Lighter, pearly-white vapour curled skyward in intervals like a heartbeat pulsing. The casement dissipated in lapping flames, only to be renewed constantly by the frame itself. The opening in the sky resonated with life in a new dimension.

Finally, I tore myself away and continued toward Astor. I couldn't help but gaze at the sky as I walked, periodically tripping over roots or clumps of long grasses. I completely forgot about the wolves at the river. Thank God I did pick up audible sounds through my earthly senses as I stepped along the spongy ground. The smashing and rolling sounded distant, yet close enough for me to decipher rushing water crashing onto a remote shoreline.

Odd, to be sure, a long-beaked silhouette suggested a lone raven perched on a dead treetop above Astor, who sat on an old stump leaning against the trunk. Like me, he was peering up at the sky. The sorrowful croak of the raven relieved me. Good, I'm still on this earth, I reasoned.

Losing interest quickly, I switched back to the flaming window in the sky. A bush plane could have easily flown through the suspended frame with room to spare. The barn-sized structure was on fire, but it held in complete silence amid flickers of fiery orange. A teardrop formation, interconnected like a fish net, hung over the bottom edge, as if ready to pull in a load of fish inside the window by an unseen force. The coarse net spiralled crystal clear like a barber shop post sign.

Once my consciousness immersed itself in this glorious apparition, time had no meaning; pain and discomfort were foreign. A sense of belonging rested supreme on my shoulders. I felt like a precious stone in the palm of our Creator, which needed no introduction.

Was Astor witnessing the same while sitting on that old tree stump? Although I did not know it then, the whole purpose of the heavenly apparition would be revealed to us at the end of the day. In short, Astor and I would be given a vision of how angels travelled from heaven to their earthly assignments to enhance the kingdom of God, young people. I cannot explain it any better, but we both understood.

As I reached Astor and sat down quietly beside him, I had tons of questions. After all, right from the beginning of our fishing trip, he had arranged for the angels to meet us here; I was sure of that. But why? Before I could ask, he cautiously slid forward, down onto his knees. He raised a hand as a signal to hold all conversation. I did for the time being. My sense of hearing alerted me to look to my right like he was. There, advancing, crawling like a bulldozer, was our mysterious boulder, which I pointed out to you this morning at the river. The large stone was shifting, scraping the ground, and creeping toward the river. The mass of granite proved to possess a relentless drive forward. Pushing and breaking away piles of debris in its path, leaving behind a levelled corridor a person could walk along without lifting his feet.

I witnessed several tree trunks fall across the path, bending, crunching, and giving way in jagged splinters before the boulder. Several grouse broke cover and split the air, batting wings, clearly terrified. That was when I saw the giant bull moose trailing behind the stone, head low as if tied to the monument. The moose had a sickening limp. No lie to you, son, on my grandmother's grave; this was what your father witnessed that day. Can I go on?

After noticing the moose lumbering along some two hundred yards away, my attention fell on furry grey backs parting tall vegetation in slow motion, silent. Even city dwellers with limited exposure to the animal kingdom would grasp the objective. The wolves were closing in for the kill. We were far enough away, however. The wolves were preoccupied with the moose and didn't appear to notice us at all. Here comes the crazy part. I swear my guardian angel nudged me to look up. Lo and behold, the same two angels, suspended in mid-air above the tree line, were dressed in camo. They wore mukluks (native winter boots) laced up to their knees. Well, yes, up in the Yukon, even for angels, there was no such thing as bare feet. Still a bit late in the season for boots, I'd say? The camo robes were buckled in the middle with a thick leather belt securing two knives in place. Songbirds flew in and out between them, frazzled, not knowing what to make of the sight, not daring to land. The raven was nowhere to be seen.

One angel stretched his arms out with pursed lips, patting the air and shushing. The two angels eyed each other, murmuring while focusing their divine attention on the ground below. Their oily, pitch-black hair parted in the middle and fell straight, tossed lazily in the breeze. They gently encouraged the injured moose with moans of endearment while scanning for hindrances on the forest floor.

Somehow, I understood that the low, carefree hum of the angels soothed the weary moose over and over again without ceasing. Dragging his backside, the encumbered bull moose smeared the now stationary boulder with his blood. The animal showing insurmountable fatigue and in dire need, stumbled over the last fallen timber before arriving at the river's clearing. The dewlap—or bell—under its chin swung low in a desperate mood. The moose's hind leg was broken above the toe hooves. The jagged leg bone protruded through the skin at a sickening angle. Embedded in dry blood, flakes of blue paint from the truck stuck to his fur.

Given Astor's blue 4x4's speed, the impact was proving fatal; something had to give. His domain would be forever altered. From now on, the bull moose's fifty-square-mile range would be infiltrated by the younger generation waiting in line. The deadly injury had attracted swarms of flies in clusters of churning black masses constantly landing on exposed pink flesh. The larva stage was already underway.

Drained of brute animal strength, near collapse and numb with pain, the moose stood there, staring far out over the river. Ten winters are old for a moose. Around the eyes and nose, tufts of white whiskers confirmed the years. The animal's lifespan was setting like the sun, dimming blood red. In his present situation, the will to fight and survive was foreign, period. With a broken leg in the middle of the wilderness, people, it was senseless. After picking up the overwhelming wolf scent, the powerful herbivore raised his mini-car-sized antlers and, by habitual instinct more than logic, attempted to shift sideways to face one bold, growling female. Alas! The swollen hind leg refused to cooperate in a swift reflex; again and again, pain flared.

You can bet your last dollar that, in the moose's prime, without injuries, if a wolf got too close, a swift sidekick to the head would send mister fang airborne, with his carcass catapulting dead on the way down. That usually discouraged other attempts, but not this time, even if the pack hadn't fully comprehended that. The giant bull-moose was in agony and could not defend itself. He stared down, wide-eyed, at his canine foes for a moment, and then the moose's muscular neck rippled as he turned to look back at the Boreal Forest, home for so many years.

The die was cast. The wolves, sensing the possibility, fidgeted, advanced, and retreated, wincing in high-pitched growls, uncertain as to the best way to proceed while pacing to and fro, to and fro. The wolves knew there could very well be a last burst of energy from the brute; if he chose to use his immense rack, an unexpected side hook to the rib cage would send a wolf flying, cannonball style.

Who will be the first to challenge? The wolves appeared to ask themselves silently. To initiate the charge head-on at a lowered, six-foot-wide bone rack fused to 2000 pounds of vengeance? Who will be the first in the pack to risk broken bones of no return? To take on that bold thrust forward without regard for life. Logic could advise not to charge until blue in the face. In this fateful hour, logic was puny and needed to go home. Only the brave, the visionary, can restore the circle of life with sheer determination, soothe hunger, return to the den, and nurse the pups.

The forest stood reverent, except for heavy breathing. A few more precious moments if the moose could endure them. One more tiny life frame to ponder, to reminisce on days of old when the king moose roamed among prehistoric relics. The wolves allowed it out of respect, perhaps, for the majestic beast towering over them. Or maybe still fearful, still cautious.

God's commission had been a success, sending two angels to round up an unfortunate moose and use the accident for good—saving the lives of Astor and me.

As we watched, the wolves closed in. His reserves depleted, the moose did not have it in him to fight for long, and the attack ended mercifully.

Of course, it would take time for the wolves to get their fill. Having descended from the treetops during the last few moments of the great beast's life, one of the angels casually walked over to us and explained the situation. He said, "Don't return to the river to fish yet. Once done eating, the pack of wolves will have to pass by there to reach their den."

"What are we supposed to do in the meantime?" asked Astor.

"For that two-hour eating frenzy," replied the angel, "I have been permitted to guide you through a flashback in time personally. God has appointed the exact period. No later than 1200 A.D. "The miracle of travelling back in time will be achieved if you can imagine, through a raven's eye, for Yahweh works in mysterious ways."

Astor and I sat on the old stump, surrounded by our fishing gear. We did not dare move or stir other conversations with our angel standing by. I wasn't sure where Astor had summoned the courage earlier, but it seemed to have dissipated now; Sheepishly, we gazed at each other, waiting for the impact, whatever that would look like. Suddenly, in a whirlwind, a cloud of red leaves lifted us in the spirit. We flew, elongated, through the eyes of the raven, and what a trip it was. I cried to Astor while stretched like a rubber band arcing across the sky, "Why are we doing this again?"

Astor's words echoed in my ears. "You will understand more when we return in two hours. There's more, a lot more-more-more..."

The traverse through the heavenly dimension was painless, although it gave me hiccups.

1200 AD

1200 AD

A memorable period for the local natives, where bow and arrow were the supreme hunting weapon of choice and flint, the champion cutting tool. Black spruce dominated the land, interrupted only by wetlands with crystal-clear lakes. Long before the Hudson Bay and North West Companies with their voyageurs, (*le coureur de bois*). Long before the railroads and before the white people panning for gold. And here we were, Astor and I, staring down at a vast wilderness. We witnessed this with our eyes while accompanied by our guardian angel guide.

A short distance below, woodland caribou with their heads lowered were engaged in a rhythm of mass grazing. The shifting brown bodies advanced meticulously, white shoulder to white shoulder, like a wall of Confederate soldiers. Like fluttering butterflies near water, bright yellow birds perched on the animals' antlers, periodically frisking their wings, ready to go.

Then, in the blink of an eye, the wiry birds shot straight up on flapping wings to dive bomb unwary insects being chased by marching hooves.

The massive herd spilled out in a carpet of shifting backsides before dipping into a valley far below, only reappearing on the other side like ants in a mist. Above, skies appeared ocean-blue with occasional puffs of white. The animals didn't seem to mind having a flock of blackbirds riding on their backs. The birds' movements instantly soothed a month-long itch with their needle-sharp claws when the group shuffled to obtain a favourable forward position. But the main attraction for the birds was to feed on protein-rich insects. Airborne flies were determined to land below the animals' runny eye ducts and around the nose discharging mucus. Because of the constant tingling caused by the relentless pests, the docile grass eaters would occasionally slip a pointy tongue inside one nostril and then the other to wipe their runny noses, which tasted salty.

Like a summer grass fire, the hooves of the advancing herd disrupted countless insects fleeing in a panic, only to be crunched by flying beaks. Nothing was left untouched, none wasted. Within the hour, most of the animals' droppings would be rounded up by dung beetles; whatever was left behind became fertilizer for spring grass. The remote hazy background rising over a snowy peak commanded caution. If Astor and I ever decided to pack a lunch at sunrise to reach the foothills before dark, wood benches would not be provided along the way; it's no walk in the park.

From our vantage point, the wildflowers swaying above endless tall grasses mimicked the swell of an ocean. Lounging above a low cloud and witnessing all, Astor and I were obliged to twist our necks like the sandhill crane to take in all the scenery. Strangely enough, we observed animals, nature, and people living independently throughout the two hours of time travel in the fourth dimension. It was like we were part of them, walking in their shoes. We felt more than heard their life stories.

In all of this, of all things, I thought about the raven. The troublesome bird was nowhere to be seen. I also thought about what Astor had said: there would be so much more after we returned to the Salmon River to fish.

1200 AD. In the dead of winter, millions of hooves are migrating thousands of miles, and causing the earth to tremble, rescuing whole villagers from starvation. Around campfires, legends of heroic hunts were cherished and preserved from one generation to another over hundreds of years.

"It came about one summer…." Now full of years, the cross-legged warrior sat around his clan, orange shadows dancing on his face. Choked by campfire smoke, the air was filled with the aroma of roasted wild game dripping in fat. Eventually, the people gathered around, dragging blankets under the stars. The constant mating calls of the frogs provided the soundtrack for the gathering.

Crawling in silence on hands and knees, determined children squeezed their temples between large knees to stare, wide-eyed, into the flames, listening to their grandfather's story and hoping to be soon fed. The astute storyteller raised his arm that held an imaginary bow and spoke and spoke. With older, presumably even hungrier children, a thought came to mind: Will Grandfather ever release the arrow so we can eat?"

Nonetheless, the effect was powerful—buck-skin-clad bodies leaned forward, engrossed, clueless, jaws agape. One probed the nearest fellow to add more wood to the fire. Sitting around the flickering flames, they felt the heat soothing, warming them inside; the air they breathed tasted smoky, which was why buzzing mosquitos had given up for the night.

But that was summer. Suddenly, without warning, we zoomed away to mid-winter while still sitting on our cloud. The situation changed drastically for Astor and me. We gasped and marvelled, our heads swivelling as we marvelled some more at the whole life experience unfolding.

Next to us, our angel announced, "Hush and listen up. Now you will witness a great ancient hunt. Memorize the events in your minds."

The Hunt

By instinct, the dogs sensed something in the air and triggered the alarm with muffled whimpering. The famished villagers caught wind of a sound. Coyotes yelping? No way, not a chance. Their human ears were long accustomed to deciphering voices in the forest. These were no four-legged creatures yelping. Hey, hey! What a welcoming, rowdy bunch, indeed. Ecstatic, their young bucks hooted success for their morning hunt by imitating wild animals. The hunting party approached in haste, creaky snowshoes pressing snow. Jumbled voices with chaotic yelping spurred each other on to greater volume. The village people turned their heads to follow the sight—arms in the air clutching horizontal bows in one hand and a chunk of meat in the other.

Astor and I felt privileged to be part of this genuine reunion celebrating a great bounty. Elders jolted out of their huts, step-dancing in sleeping moccasins. Some of the moves were pretty impressive. The raven showed up unannounced, rehearsing croaks while ruffling feathers from beak to tail to get people's attention. The raven wasn't done yet. He relieved himself, leaving a large pile of excrement before flying to his feeding post place by the villagers. The raven did that occasionally for no explicit reason. Some said vegetation would not grow on that spot for at least three years; it was disgusting and rude. Nonetheless, it did not matter; in times of extreme, no one needed to be left behind; all were welcome to partake in the villagers' good fortune. No exclusions.

Reduced to a handful, the young and the enduring hunters rushed back ahead of the others to the villagers, desperate for food. While walking, they chewed raw meat in a deliberate, sluggish fashion. This allowed their empty digestive systems to adjust for heavy food intake. Revived physical strength was like an instant miracle. Faces glowed with broad smiles, eyes sparkled, and the whole body leaped forward crying out, "We made a kill! A *moose*! We've got provisions to last the rest of the winter. Eat the meagre portions you stored for tomorrow," they counselled, "Because …" a pause, a body arced back as the speaker slapped his stomach with both hands, "… tonight we eat until we drop."

The fruitful hunters had prime time on stage; everyone wanted to hear their stories. Who made the kill? Where? How many arrows?

A successful hunter's arm propped vertically. "Gather your sleds; I'll show you the way. Follow me. We must haul toboggan loads of meat back before nightfall, as the wolves won't wait till morning. In the meantime, send the children out; we can use extra firewood." Under normal conditions, several would have called to harness the dogs, but most had been consumed before the new moon. They'd kept a handful of the best canine to regenerate the hauling pack, hopefully, soon, a wise decision approved in the last village council meeting.

That day, the dogs' futures were restored; they could be fruitful again and multiply. Hand-picked volunteers took care of sowing together old, worn-out hides and fabricating a large, jagged circle blanket with a bottom and top cover. With winter night temperatures dropping to -30 Celsius, sheltering the remaining dogs from the cold remained crucial.

After gathering arms full, the children stuffed dry beaver grass inside the blankets and, to be safe, a foot thick on the roof. The snow didn't even melt on top. No dog coaxing was necessary to make them crawl under two sheets of fur padded with dry beaver grass. The weary dogs had wasted away to loosen bags of living bones, not fit to lift their bodies, let alone pull a load of meat on a toboggan.

Astor and I could detect paws scratching hide at the doghouse with the occasional whimper. The crude but warm doghouse sanctuary was spread under a thick-limbed spruce tree. With noses resting on the outer fur, hunger was all the dogs knew. Misery was evident in their eyes. Children would often come to report conditions, and hand feed their meagre portions prepared by the adults in a warm liquid. A regular attendant was Turtle-shell, the man-child. Born premature and frail, or so it seemed at first. Just by looking at Turtle-shell feeding the dog, Astor and I instantly recognized every detail about his life. For His good pleasure, The Holy Spirit assisted in mysterious ways.

This is what happened. Early on in puberty, Turtle-shell's spine grew abnormally. In modern-day medicine, it has a name—Scheuermann's Kyphosis. The front of the spine doesn't grow as fast as the back of the spine, causing vertebrae to wedge together. The unfortunate child becomes stooped, bending forward. When walking, the head went loose and fell on his chest. When he was a newborn, the stout hunters from the village learned of Turtle-shell's fragile nature. They were too eager with their predictions, vouchsafing, "The child won't last one winter."

Later on, they had to correct themselves. "Two winters" Whoops again. "Four winters?" Turtle-shell made liars of them all; he had twelve winters under his turtle neck and was still going strong, although joining hunting adventures was out of the question.

Looking at the man-boy shadow walking around in the evening, his body contour appeared like a turtle walking upright. Hence the name: Turtle-shell. "Don't you mind," said Turtle-shell's sensible mother. "There are things just as important for a village, like gathering firewood."

Turtle-shell became a professional wood gatherer for life, whereas other children, after eight winters, progressed onto other growing-up skills. When firewood surfaced as a concern at the evening counsel, a brisk elder commented, "Send Turtle-shell ahead of the group. That man-boy can find firewood in a pile of rocks." The jubilant laugh that followed had some truth in it. Those men felt awkward for their rash predictions of Turtle-shell's early death and proud of him for beating the odds. They wanted to make up for their words however they could and leave the past behind.

That weekly firewood gathering was terrific but not Turtle-shell's true passion. The miniature forest world was Turtle-shell's true love—insects like the carpenter-ant, beetles, bumblebees, and spiders. Also, his favourite feathered friend—you might have guessed that one—was the hummingbird.

In constant view of the village, Turtle-shell spent hours rummaging the forest floor and creeping along, inches from the ground, to observe an insect's daily activity with fascination. Last spring, he'd spotted two male beetles sparring for a female. "Let's add another male beetle into the mix and see what happens," thought the mischievous Turtle-shell. A hand-sized wood spider was his next observatory site, flicking a string on her web to reel in her gullible opponent. Of course, the spider pulled strings in vain; the unsuspecting opponent was the face of Turtle-shell, smiling while disrupting the web with a long, skinny stick.

When those few interfering village people observed the awkward man-boy walking through the woods with a stooped back, they whispered to each other with a hand to the mouth, saying, "His posture looks like the contour of a turtle." They would ask, "Is it painful when you walk?" Turtle-shell ignored all short-sighted inquiries and walked away. Specifically, Turtle-shell loved the miniature world for a good reason—the tiny creatures carried out their everyday lives without meddling in other people's affairs, never commenting behind anyone's back. Besides, if an insect like the beetle did decide to turn and have a look at Turtle-shell, what the beetle saw was a giant and nothing else.

Enough was enough. This one time, he was determined to fight back.

It needed careful planning to remedy the situation. Older boys from the village made fun of Turtle-shell being different. One day in late fall, near the village, he discovered a deer carcass, half eaten by a bear and buried in leaves. The man-boy was a genuine, mind-boggling opportunist. Without anyone's consent, he dragged the carcass back to his village. When the surprised posse of boys intercepted him at the village fire, they asked, "Where did you get the deer Turtle-shell, and why is it half eaten?"

Turtle-shell scratched his jaw briefly before answering nonchalantly, "I was standing on top of the crow's cliff at the river and saw a deer drinking below. I aimed carefully, threw down a large stone, and broke his neck. Then, while I was dragging the deer back to the village, a bear blocked my path and wouldn't let me pass. We talked for a while concerning our odd predicament. At the end of our conversation, we became brothers and arrived at a compromise. I said you could eat half the deer and leave our village the other half; that way, we can both walk away with a full stomach. I will also put my necklace around your neck as a sign for my village not to hunt you.

"The bear agreed eagerly by grunting with his head shifting sideways, up and down, and his lips curled up to smile at me. So, I sat on a stump until old brother bear was done eating his half of the deer, and now, here I am."

The posse of boys gawked at each other, terrified. From that day forward, young and older adults greatly respected Turtle-shell. Who wouldn't, since he has an old friend to fight battles with, and that old friend is a black bear?

Back to the starving dogs. For hours, Turtle-shell would kneel on dry mats at the enclosure, petting the dogs with the other children. Placing one sorrowful head in his lap and then the next, he would gently stroke the unbelievably loose skin while feeding the animal. "Give them warm water, as much as they want," a grown-up would advise. But Turtle-shell, the dog whisperer, knew they needed much more than water; the dogs urgently required a reddish substance, meat. Aye! Growing only big enough to do children's work, he understood the hapless creatures too well. All children cared deeply. Why did grown-ups think little ones needed to grow big before making a difference? Some so-called mature people were too preoccupied to notice, but, for hours at a time, children pinched blood-sucking flees off the starving dogs, preserving precious energy and easing irritation. The children also parted the dog's soft fur to pick out brambles that clumped the fur and let the cold in, and they rubbed aching muscles at length to circulate the blood. When no one was around, Turtle-shell spoke into the downcast ears with his cupped hands, whispering words of encouragement.

"Hold on a little longer, my four-legged companions, and don't worry, my blue and brown-eyed friend. I won't let the village people eat you. Fresh meat will be tossed on the snow for you soon." Turtle-shell stuck a hand in front of his favourite dog, Runner. "Here, I stole a nibble for you, Runner, so you won't forget what meat tastes like."

The rambunctious pup snatched the morsel instantly and licked his lips, asking for more. Turtle-shell rested a hand on his head. "Be patient, my courageous fellow. Our village made a large kill this morning. The hour of deliverance is at hand."

Tracking back to the kill zone can be accomplished blindfolded. It had been observed as toddlers, practiced as young boys, talked about in groups and supervised by parents and grandparents to no end. Nobody needed instructions. A party with the most vigour left first; men and women went ahead in snowshoes to pack down a narrow runway, providing a stable base for loaded toboggans. Other groups followed minutes behind, towing empty sleds and backpacks. The thin, light strap made of moose hide came attached to the front corners of the sled's frame. Shaping to the body's contours in a loop, it curved around the back of a person's neck and under the armpits. With this method of hauling, the arms and hands were left free to protect the eyes from branches whipping back and to grip a bow-and-arrow if needed.

The people walked in a forward-leaning posture so the legs and body weight could do most of the pulling. This technique allowed a person to walk all day, pulling a considerable load on a toboggan with minimum energy. Most importantly, they would not perspire heavily along the way and then, being the middle of winter, foolishly sit alone to rest, fall asleep, and freeze.

Spirits flew high on the trail. "Ho-ho-ho, here we walk, not too slow, with our sleds ready to go. Yes, it is moose meat that we tow, ho-ho-ho, don't you know?" The person behind was supposed to answer in a rhyming reply. The good-natured duets soon fall apart, revealing complete delinquency in poetry

Occasionally, a fist went up to the face, clutching a piece of the meat distributed by the first arrivals in the village. The side of the mouth closed tight against their thumb and index finger, liquid running dark red down to the wrist—multiple vitamins overload from a chunk of raw moose liver or heart. Like magic, bellies gurgled, churning warmth outwardly, releasing loud and unpleasant burps.

Drowsiness and fatigue melted away. Their arms felt like a seabird's open wings high on the cliff, their spirits urging them to drop and soar over blue skies. Tonight, my friends, the river people, young and old, would dance among campfires, jubilant. Yesterday's sorrows will vanish; tomorrow brings clear skies and sunshine to boot. You could rest assured that the good news would spread like wildfire. Neighbouring villagers from a two-sun-up walk, would stream in like shabby muskrats out of water. From every direction— north, south, east, and west—they would arrive, out of courtesy bearing fine pairs of moccasins and baskets of renowned handiwork. Children especially would be given ornaments and dolls to play with.

A few would show up unprepared and empty-handed. The awkward arrival for those unfortunates would be shoved aside by the welcoming committee with shouts to come near, followed by a manly embrace that popped the eyes out. They had all been there; no point in making a fuss or shaming the newcomers in dire need. "Glad that you came, brother. Have a seat, rest, and then we eat."

The Salmon River Valley and the Mountain of Tear's villagers would appear like a herd of wood caribou breaking out in a storm. Sharing one's good fortune with neighbouring villagers would have no bounds. Shouting and cries of laughter trailing among sparse tree trunks would traverse up to the goats' plateau. Villagers eager to socialize stood tall, wondering who would come out their way. Over and over, they welcomed the ones streaming in. "Good to see you; it's been too long. Please celebrate with us.

Tell us news from afar; we have delightful hunting stories."

Thigh muscles struggled to bend the knee. Mukluks dragging along the trail went sloppy, clumps of snow melting down to bare ankles were turning freezing red. The urgency to reach the village drove them on. Boots would be the first to come off and hung up to dry. What other remedy could satisfy but time and rest? The remaining hunting party, exhausted, made its way back around campfires. The well-deserved reward for providers was to see the relief on the children's faces, and the crack of a smile out of those who had suffered from prolonged hunger. Pure joy. All was well.

Some astute hunters, the animal trackers who did most of the open-range canvassing, headed inside the family hut and crashed flat out. The siblings invented a game out of it, pulling off Pop's mukluks while he was fast asleep and hanging them on the porch to dry. One older boy stood apart in the hunters' path, clutching a new bow with both hands. The sturdy individual spent hours in the evening by the campfire. He used chars of flint to scrape and shape his precious bow-and-arrow and then filled his birch-bark quiver with genuine hunting arrows. The shoulder-height wood shaft had dried for two seasons. The natives preferred one wood species to shape a bow—the massive black ash tree found in lowlands with a smooth trunk growth equivalent to a man's height. This ensured unified wood grain without any knots or defects that could flex and whip back without breaking.

They rarely cut the tree down because, with a flint axe, they would be faced with days of chipping away like a beaver; the work was painstakingly demanding. They commonly used a flint axe with handfuls of flint wedges. The group started by carving a lateral groove roughly a bow's length. Then, by driving in flint wedges, they gradually peeled away a thick wood slab, approximately the width and thickness of a man's wrist. Surprisingly, the massive tree usually survived the onslaught for future visits.

The young apprentice had recently finalized waterproofing the smooth, flexible shaft with bear grease. Brightly coloured goodwill hunting strands had been fastened at the tips of the bow. The young craftsmen had taken precautions to wet and then wrap thin deer hide over the centred handle for a comfortable hand grip, adding durability while embedding a precise edge, not too high, not too low, for the arrow to rest on. The young man-warrior-soon-to-be stood on the trail. He fixed dark eyes forward, budging for no one, staring intensely. With plans activated, he spoke to himself in a whisper. "My new birch bark quiver filled with arrows sticking out from the back; surely my father's brother will notice that."

The frown on his young face never left him; mark the day, that time, young age did not flinch, did not step aside; after all, it was part of the plan. The seasoned hunter approaching held a smile and looked away to distance himself from the determined boy blocking his path. Even wiping his face with an open hand didn't prevent the corner of his mouth from curling. Pretending nothing was amiss, the relative stepped aside and walked around the steadfast youth, decorated head to toe with his hunting gear.

While passing, the hunter extended his arm to shake the lad's shoulder for signs of readiness. He wasn't disappointed. No words were exchanged, but the determined boy understood. *One day soon, you will join our hunting party.* The boy took a deep breath, relieved that no confrontation had been necessary. On the contrary, the young hunter would find approval to be included very soon among his people.

Walking back to his hut, he felt the urge to jump and click his heels, ready to fly on wings. He couldn't wait to tell his friends.

The Daughter's Father

A father arriving from the hunt sprang to life when noticing his children standing attentively in a row outside their hut. People knew the comical father of many daughters who cramped stomachs at the campfire with his lavish stories; today was no exception. His arms flew open, and he stood cross-eyed and absurd, with fingers pointing at the clouds. He gawked, a look of astonishment on his face, replete with bulging eyes, and his head jerked back as if gripped by monstrous fear; a low grunt resonated for the theatrical. The droll father stood this way for two minutes in front of the young girls without speech. For the awestruck youth, two minutes was an eternity.

They all cried out, thoughts and voices muddled with terror. "What happened, Papa? What did you see while hunting in the woods; tell us, what did you see?"

The father prolonged his answer by sniffing the air with a stretched neck. Finally, he spoke.

"I saw… I saw the great beast standing so close I could smell his breath." Father dearest continued with his nostrils flaring, sniffing the air wide-eyed but more profoundly this time.

"With my longbow pulled to the ear, trembling, your father's arrows plunged through his big heart. Broad as a river was the moose chest; the feathers of my arrows disappeared in his fur one after the other— *froush... froush... froush*. Along with suction-sound effects, the animated father used his index finger to imitate arrows striking his chest, one-two-three, while his knees buckled.

"Before falling, the mountain moose shifted to one side, blocking the whole sun, for the day turned to nighttime. His humongous head fell and fell, raining down squirrels and pinecones from the treetops. A moose growing that tall, oh! I wouldn't be surprised if he needed to stoop under a full moon when walking by. Before the beast finally crashed to the ground with a thunderous thud, your father had a moment to smoke the pipe. This is no lie to you, my furry musk-washes. Once spread out to dry, the moose hide will be big enough to build three canoes and one large blanket for four button-nosed musk-washes to sleep under."

A regiment of fidgeting legs couldn't hold the suspense any longer, and a mishmash of feet dispersed amid shouts of adventure. The girls ran in circles, hopping like jackrabbits spooked by the bushy tail of a fox. All the while, energetic little bodies imitated their father's gestures, arms flailing up and down. Oh? With impeccable timing, a grey owl joined the show. Hoot. Hoot. The forest was filled with magical danger—who knew what lurked behind that tree or this rock? Hoot. Hoot.

"Papa, Papa, I want to sleep under the moose blanket. No. Let me. No, me-me."

"Don't you fuss, my fidgeting duck-tails? After stuffing your bellies with moose meat tonight, you, my little girls, will sleep through a herd of wood caribou thundering through our village."

Curtains closed; the stage play was over. After one or two huffs for clearing air passages, captain father frowned amiably, both arms directing his young female crew. "Now quickly, my daughters, gather firewood, take out the sitting mats, cut green alder sticks for roasting, and get the family pot ready for boiling water; we need to prepare warm moose broth for your grandma. Was she up this morning?" After the short inquiry, Father's voice hushed as he stared towards the hut where Grandmother slept, remembering the owl's hoot. The father felt the owl was a bad omen; it represented night darkness where a person rested forever. Or so some said.

The Angel

During that time, Astor and I sat on a plush sofa cloud above the treetops, overlooking the village. Our guardian angel stood beside us, responding to our questions and every need. I had a glass of wine in my hand, which I enjoyed very much. Astor, being an Alcoholics Anonymous (AA) member for 40 years, had a bowl of grapes, and they looked delicious. I was proud of Astor being true to his sobriety even while travelling in a heavenly dimension. More for fun than curiosity, I asked our angel guide what year the wine was.

He smirked at me and said, "We kept some of it from the wedding, so 30 AD."

My eyes widened, and I glanced at Astor. He raised his shoulders and kept eating grapes. I wasn't sure if our angel was pulling my leg or not. But, just in case, I tipped my wine glass lightly in both hands and cautiously rolled the dark purple liquid around the glass while staring at it in wonder. When I stopped, I gently raised the glass to my lips and sipped, careful not to waste a drop.

Without warning, the angel stretched his arm out to point at a hut below, the grandmother's hut, and then spoke with authority.

"Gird yourself and pay attention. The Spirit will carry both of you gents inside the hut. You will be completely transparent in the villagers' epoch. When you find yourselves sitting cross-legged around the campfire, remain watchful for a time; study and remember the events."

Astor and I were excited about the close contact, the intimacy, and the privilege of witnessing the everyday life of ancient people in the Yukon. Did they have the same dreams and hopes as modern civilization? As I grew conscious of my body stretching towards the hut, I asked our angel guide, "Is it possible to have more grapes and wine, please?"

Grandmother's Bed

ours later, Willow, the oldest of the four girls, had the honour of carrying steaming broth to her grandmother. The warmth soothed her palms when holding the wooden bowl with both hands, although the aroma disturbed Willow's stomach. Born to be slim, her delicate frame slumped forward as she entered the hut backwards. By routine, her head tipped sideways as she eyed the trinkets suspended on thin strings tied to the ceiling framing poles. As she entered, the dangling miniature animal figures brushed haphazardly across her body and tapped against each other. No, under her watchful eye, none would dip into her precious hot liquid.

The three younger sisters followed her inside, one after the other, as if tied by a rope. Their grandma's sleeping area was to the right. Willow stood inside, blinking; it did not help—she could hardly detect the intertwined saplings. The hand-width-high raised bedframe was constructed above ground to aid air circulation, thus lessening the possibility of mouldy bedding. A thick layer of cedar boughs lay interlocked on top of the frame. Dark forest-green branches flowed over the rectangle bed frame, curving downward at the ends in a plush diamond pattern fit for a queen. The strong pine smell discouraged insects.

On top of the branches, three white sheepskins had been sown together with the wool outward. The arctic blanket overflowed on all sides with the familiar contours of the animal's back legs and neck area. The top cover provided heat to the body while also muffling sound. The narrow strips looped at the edges were functional handles for tugging the blanket over the head, a straightforward way of combatting winter at midnight after the fire went out.

More long fur bedding from different animals, such as wolves, was stuffed with smoke-dried moss (to kill bugs) and rolled up as pillows. Grandma used them to prop herself on one elbow, as people did at the dinner table in Jesus' time. Now Grandmother could sip her moose broth and tell stories simultaneously without excuses.

Stretched out and resting on her elbow, tangled grey hair falling around her face, the aged woman retained a stooped posture while eying the steaming broth only an arm's length away. In her famished state, the aroma of cooked moose broth triggered gurgling in her stomach. The scuffling feet of her granddaughter Willow had crept closer cautiously. The bedding area lay immersed in darkness, and Willow knew precisely why. Squinting across the interior patterns of grey, her eyes gravitated to the centre of the dirt floor. She had no trouble distinguishing a dim pile of coals. That wouldn't do. Her housekeeping instincts were activated. Standing behind in darkness, a faint but purposeful side movement towards her sisters was enough.

Like teamwork without pomp, the task was accomplished in silence and efficiently; the sisters added more wood to the fire in the hut's centre. The girls knew firewood was a precious commodity, so stoking a fire was not a haphazard, throw-it-in affair. They took precautions to heap the coals and carefully placed each chunk of firewood, leaning around the red embers like a teepee. That would rouse the flames to lick the wood surface upward, creating a tall, flaming torch. The heat from cooking fires was always welcome inside a hut, but the flames also increased light.

Willow cried out, "Grandma, Grandma… are you sleeping?"

"What a question." Grandma groaned and pressed a hand to her sunken abdomen. "My ravaged stomach won't allow sleep." Ceiling shadows performed leaping flares over the sheep blanket. Stirring, moaning, a body form shifted to adjust her braced left shoulder afresh. Eyelids opened, reflecting black pearls. Her seasons were numerous—sixty winters. Her smile was wreathed in permanent, deep-seated wrinkles. With several wakening headshakes, frazzled grey hair cascaded over beddings. The olive brown skin, darkened from years in the open country, glowed in the firelight.

As a young girl, her beauty had been equal to a river princess. Willow was her favourite granddaughter. The little girl was a wide-eyed bundle of energy who questioned life to the moon and back. "What's you asking?" Grandma would enquire multiple times throughout the day. No coaxing was needed for help, for the villagers understood that Willow carried her heart on her sleeve. Even so, her sensitivity left the bubbly child open to criticism.

Running with open arms to Grandma, she would squeeze the aged body and ask, sorrow in her voice, "Why? Oh, why are they being cruel to me, Grandma? Willow would describe some exasperating incident with no end in sight. Numerous times, as Grandma crouched near, her grey head leaned to one side, her face portraying serious concern for Willow's mysterious calamity. The child's face would soon open in a wide smile.

Standing at a crossroads with a child was all it took to reassure a tender soul that the sky would not fall on Willow or Grandma today. Grandma had prophesied that Willow's whirlwind emotions were precious gifts of the Great Spirit. Speaking the truth in a shout was primarily assigned to chief warriors and unique little girls like her. At four years old, she had received the prophecy of her grandma and never questioned it. "When you join hurtful activities," Grandma would quote, pointing at the forest, "dragging your feet in the woods only invites dead leaves in your home; no healing will come from that. Put your house in order, sweep out the dead leaves, and learn from your mistakes. They will make you grow stronger. Remember," Grandmother shared one of her favourite quotes, "if you hide inside your shell like a turtle, the adversary will treat you like one and flip you over and laugh at you."

Memories flitted through Willow's mind as she lowered herself to the ground beside the grey woman's bed.

"Yes, yes, my busy munchkins, how can I not be awake? I can smell that moose broth across the village."

A radiant smile spread across Grandmother's face—a smile where facial muscles had given up holding back the years, a loving smile to gravitate near when others were too busy. Who could resist? Sitting tight, listening to stories, and eating sweets were cherished recollections of going to Grandma's. In chaotic times, aged serenity drew little ones seeking comfort. A restless toddler sitting close to Grandma and fidgeting received her full attention. The reproach that pricked the heart of an infant would not surface there. *Go on, rest your sleepy head as a kind hand gently strokes your hair.*

Oh, all you grandmothers, your mysterious melodies have lifted our souls to faraway lands. When darkness comes, bedtime stories leave us smiling from the beginning to fast asleep, filling our yearnings with treasures to keep. "Oh yes, it is rumoured that little people build their houses inside hollowed mushrooms, and oh yes, once tall and handsome was the prince warrior…."

When Willow laid her head on the soft blanket, past occurrences directed her to slide an open hand separating her cheek and blanket. That pesky Dall sheep fleece would tickle her nose without mercy if she didn't. At first, Willow felt the vibration in her ear, a deep murmuring, and then a repetitive melody of thanksgiving blending higher and higher filled the atmosphere. With her mouth closed in reverence, Grandma mainly sang through her nose.

"Thankful are we, oh! Great Spirit in teaching us to be watchful of evil encounters. You have helped to overcome our difficulties with the hunt. You chase hunger out of our homes like spring migration. You renew our strength with Living Water. Thankful are we, oh! Great Spirit…" After giving thanks, Grandmother lifted her bowl with both hands and drank cautiously, eyes shut, moaning hungry noises between breaths. Mmm… mmm.

Mountain of Tears

"**P**lease tell us a story, Grandma—the story of The Mountain of Tears." Four little girls were eager to hear Grandmother's story. The legend has been narrated numerous times in the past centuries with diverse approaches and was forever treasured and requested again and again. Feigning a sour expression, Grandma looked both ways as if caught like a rabbit in a fence, although she loved every moment. She released a deep nasal sigh and held the stage as she considered whether she would agree. After all, they had brought her a bowl of warm moose broth and stoked the fire; what else could a grandmother possibly need?

The youngest dark-haired beauty nodded to reinforce their request and elbowed her sisters to perform the same innocent-faced plea. *Let's keep convincing Grandma; we can't give up now.* A rabbit could only throw himself against the fence so many times. In the end, the long-eared one must accept his fate. Through it all, Grandma was proud of her grandchildren's conduct. Walking over to someone and asking without enquiring about their well-being was not polite in their culture. "Have you eaten today?" Or "Do you need provision for your travels?" At the very least, they should talk about things of the day. Her grandchildren did much more; they brought lifesaving, nutritious food and increased light and warmth to the hut. There was no doubt in her mind that they were truly exceptional children.

The empty bowl still cupped in her hand, now relaxed to rest on fur. The grandmother's elongated face traversed another dimension. The warm, nutritious broth had given her instant energy to navigate the narrow road less travelled. The dark eyes drew back in a mist. A long breath filled her lungs, necessary to extend her thoughts. Her Grandmother spoke as though she sat on winter ice in the dead of night waiting for the white bear; her body did not tweak once the whole time. For the girls, staring in complete fascination, it was eerie to watch.

Grandmother spoke. "A long, long time ago, a tremendous sacred mountain stood among our people. It was called The Mountain of Tears. Many people from far away (2 full moons of canoe paddling away) came to hunt within her graceful slopes and below the foothills. Many came by the river like herds of caribou to congregate and trade. Tall rocks stood along the river near the Mountain of Tears to form a protected bay for the canoes, and a colony of sea birds nested on top. The white and black birds flew above, intercepting each other and screeching all day while fishing in the river.

"What a joy to trade and load heavy canoes and then swiftly paddle back to separate villages instead of meagre loads on packing dogs for the long, treacherous trails on land. The elders called these the good old days. For centuries in seasons, the Mountain area was talked about in songs and legends portraying dramatic hunts. If people stood on the crow's nesting side of the riverbank, young and old saw how the name came to be. Standing there looking at the mountain halfway up the steep side of the precipice, the spectacle came into view.

"The underground stream divided by a ceiling column punctured the side of the mountain and cascaded down in plumes of white spray, expanding as it fell. Below, at the foothill, the water swirled and thundered into a large, boiling pot. Thick mist rose day and night, blurring the treetops. Standing elevated at the crow's nest, as I mentioned, the cavern appeared like two dark eyes with water pouring out the base. It gave the impression that the mountain was crying all the time. Nature's wonder could be seen during the day and heard at night if close enough. And this was why the people called it The Mountain of Tears.

"The place still stands with us today, with a village nearby bearing the same name. Oh, people still travel past every summer; except now, the cascading waters are gone. Steppingstones for eagles' nests that used to reach the clouds are no longer. Because of that dreadful day, the young people no longer recognize the hunting ground. Only remnants of black craggy stone mounds, loose sand, and sparse vegetation are visible. Herds of grass-eating dwellers are a thing of the past. At the centre, where the Mountain of Tears stood, a circular turquoise body of water lies tranquil with no bottom. 'What happened here?' the young ones occasionally ask as they walk by. After so many years, the elders' answers have become muddled, depending on whom you ask. This is the most common explanation.

"A star got angry at the sun one night and, for attention, threw down a huge stone dragging its tail. When the massive rock struck the earth, an explosion followed with much disruption. The star felt remorse and tried to hide his tantrum by plugging the hole with water. After the star's outburst, the clouds grumbled for days on end, chastising the night star for his mysterious rage and poor judgment. 'Oh!' say the young ones, intrigued; the elders leave it at that. Of course, that explanation is far away from the truth."

"Oh! Why? Grandma, why is it gone? What happened to the mountain?"

Being the oldest of the girls, Willow spoke for all of them. They stood covered from head to toe in a soft deerskin that plied to their young bodies. Shiny, black hair traced their shoulders before falling loose below the waist. As an oil painting, the radiating dark eyes with button noses glowing in the shimmering plumes of orange would auction priceless. From doing chores, playing, and sharing sleeping quarters, the girls usually perceived each other's thoughts. When standing close to a warm fire in the hut's centre, hearts grew tender for storytelling. Like sea sponges, with lips parted, the absorbent young minds could receive and dish out enquiries to the sea and back and back again. Okay, brace yourself, Grandma.

"How many winters' ago, Grandma? When you were a little girl?"

The question made Grandma bite her lip and perform a deliberate head shake. While her shoulders swayed gently, trinkets clicked on strings above her bed. She closed her eyes to answer with pursed lips, "No, no." Wrinkled fingers tucked a clump of grey hair behind her ear. Then Grandma lifted the arm that didn't hold the wooden bowl and stretched and stretched as far as she could to demonstrate the ancient past. From her plush bed arrangement, she spoke again. "No, children, many winters before your grandma was born. As long as it takes for the seed of black spruce to fall on the ground and grow until you cannot wrap your arms around to touch your fingers. That's how long ago. Now then, my skittish chipmunks, no more interruptions. Listen well and take stock, asking yourself why? Why did the Mountain of Tears disappear, never to be seen again? How did she renounce her birthright for eagles to nest on her flanks? And how did the mountain lose the favour of bathing in the clouds, humbled to the point where reptiles crawled up on the tiny mounds to soak in the sun? If you have ears to hear, change how to learn to conduct your own lives." One bony finger pointed to the sky without looking. "Only if you have ears to hear."

She paused. "But first," quipped Grandma, "we need more wood on the fire."

What? She was doing it again. The little girls scowled at each other, baffled. A few low grunts escaped the mix, curiously manly for such tiny noses. They were not amused. Grandma was exercising her rights as a storyteller that went back centuries—intermission at a climax in the tale to make people fetch or do things for you; it has a measure of power and personal satisfaction. Nonetheless, the storyteller walks a fine line. Don't push your luck, Grandma; the girls may lose interest and leave you talking to the hut. It was a delicate balance, and the sage mother of many grandchildren had it down to a test-tube science.

Okay! Little hands added more wood to the fire—a small price to pay, but that was it—no more. The four stood, leaning forward, closer now and glaring with arms crossed over their chests. None spoke a word. Grandma concluded that it was time to resume her story.

"Close your eyes, my two pairs of doves. Drift back beyond dancing colours in the sky. Envision an aged mountain hooded white and sloping down onto jagged rocks. Blades of grass so tall people had to stretch their hands to touch their seedlings—an excellent basket weaver's paradise. After tumbling over rock cliffs, the crystal-clear water parts creating stony creeks rippling through the valley. Along the way, the stream branches out to even smaller rivulets. Shrubs loaded with fruit grew thick along the banks. In the fall, birds form living clouds landing and feeding. Great herds of caribou gathered, grazing throughout the summer months. Still, the most noticeable creatures that had settled on the Mountain of Tears were the well-known, often-talked-about groundhogs. They were so plentiful that a person could walk around the mountain, and his every other step would be over a groundhog burrow. A resourceful planner and a well-organized creature to behold, indeed.

"Then, one day, the destruction began, and none would have imagined. No one realized that this particular day was the beginning of the end; although a seemingly ordinary, peaceful day, before it ended, a judgment would fall from the sky, and none would escape. And it all started with a thought. To be truthful, a selfish thought.

"One day, a small group left their burrows on the prairie and took it upon themselves to excavate their dens higher on the Mountain of Tears. When other groundhogs asked why, they explained they wanted a better view of the valley below. The others didn't want to be left behind, so they reasoned with each other.

"'We want to enjoy a view of the valley also. Hey! Why don't we go up the Mountain of Tears and dig new homes for ourselves?' Oblivious to the danger, a crowd committed themselves to digging new homes. And dig they did, even higher than the water fell on the Mountain of Tears. This happened for numerous summers, arguing and bickering for a higher location to establish a dugout. Each phase of burrows was excavated higher and higher into the mountain's flank.

To the skeptics, the practice was vigorously justified by the diggers, who repeated day and night, 'The view of the valley!'

"They kept digging until the heights produced only sparse grass growth, and the distance to the valley stretched farther and farther away. The mountain's altitude compounded matters; cold and windy meant they had to dig deeper and carve out large underground rooms to store food for the winter and keep them warm at night. That brought long hours with waning energy. Back and forth, they journeyed from their lofty burrows high up on the mountain and back to the grassland below. Constant stacking and harvesting green plants to store in winter chambers for food evolved into a labour-intensive occupation. To add insult to injuries, the uphill paths twisted narrow and treacherous for travellers. Personal injuries mounted, and seasons passed. Like unruly children growing older, they forgot their joyful upbringing. Why they lived in deep burrows so high on the mountain could no longer be justified. The madness became a ritual no one questioned, a living lie cultivated for years as truth.

"Only a remnant perceived the inevitable at the time, and those few were brushed aside as old fools out of date with the new. Preoccupied with hauling food and expanding their sleeping quarters, the groundhogs shut their hearts to kinship. No time to visit neighbours for a spell or to groom each other's fur for parasites. (Whistle-whistle!) Not enough time. No time to digest, stretch, bathe in the afternoon sun, or rest. Joints and muscles ached to high heavens constantly. Therefore, there was no time for guard duty, which resulted in heated disagreements.

"Not everyone pranced up and down the mountain like a peacock. Scattered families with old leaders remained on the grassy plain. Season after season, the insanity and the absurd activities were pointed out, warnings filling the air like a desert storm. 'Whistle-whistle. Come down from the mountain, you that are heavily burdened,' the sage urged. 'Come back to the green valley where peaceful streams flow abundantly in the land. Come,' the elders cried, 'return to the open prairie where days are reflective and burdens light.'

"The groundhogs did not lend an ear to counsel. With time, their habits were seared in sorrow; they were overwhelmed by enormous burrows to upkeep. The digging and the food hauling were never-ending. They took possession of their grief, nurtured and cradled it like a newborn so that it grew and took residence in their souls. Alas! All their misfortune was self-inflicted; in vain, they presumed a preferred view of the valley would fill all their needs. As you will soon find out, my busy musquashes," concluded Grandma. "The groundhogs that wanted to elevate their lives, in the end, lost them.

"One day (in the blink of an eye) the Mountain of Tears disintegrated into a pile of dust—a sole, catastrophic conclusion unheard of by people of old. The mountain's honeycomb structure, dug out by multitudes of groundhogs, led to total collapse. The industrious creatures had developed interconnected tunnels excavated throughout the mountain's outer crust. Like an avalanche, the mountain peaks gradually converted into overload. First, the groundhogs witnessed herds of grass eaters stampeding far from the Mountain of Tears. Seconds later, the birds stopped singing. Stupefied, the groundhogs felt slight tremors through their paws. At first, no more than ripples in a puddle. Suddenly (in the blink of an eye) the Mountain of Tears spat rocks arcing in the sky like squash seeds. The roaring underground volcano bellowed, ejecting cannon balls piercing black clouds of debris expanding-rising-rising. Earth exploded from all directions in shades of grumbling darkness. Everything that had initially stood like granite, liquefied. The earth came alive to unravel in a slow stream. Daylight turned to choke night dust.

"'Oh my God! We are like ants,' concluded the flabbergasted groundhogs. 'Save us.' They stared at the Mountain of Tears disappearing in front of their eyes. Shocked to pieces, they crouched with their front paws performing a nerve-racking rubbing over the nose. Too late. Deranged eyes stared without basic instincts clueing in. Again, much too late. With the mind frozen in disbelief, the sense of smell was slow to raise a red flag. It was time to run-run. Even when racing full tilt with their chins scraping grassroots, there was no less forgiving creature as 'an earthquake.' Choking fumes invaded their throats. All over, groundhogs tumbled by the hundreds, got up and plunged headlong to get away from the chaotic nightmare convulsing from the centre of the mountain.

"Hark! A creature's spine is being thrust from behind by a one-ton boulder, a flash, the bones shattered, flat-darkness. Multitudes of groundhogs perished; young and old were crushed or buried alive. Even the ones that resided far below the Mountain of Tears, as bone-crushing boulders appeared out of nowhere, pounding the soil, bang! Bang. Enclosed by a cloud of debris mixed with hunks of wood, the boulders pulverized everything in their path—grass, trees, ants, flesh, and blood.

"Within the hour, wolves, foxes, and vultures infiltrated the area for a great feast. Bathed in confidence, a congress of ravens circled lazily above, their sporadic croaks bouncing off fresh, unmarked graves from the devastated valley below. Twitching with tongues hanging, the opportunistic coyotes sat about in groups, waiting for the dust to clear. The lame didn't go far. The Mountain of Tears was obliterated from the land, never to recover. The surviving groundhogs were so distraught by the disaster that it took years to recount the atrocity.

"'There was a dark time when the earth's centre burst open,' they would lament. Oh yes, they had plenty of regrets. 'What if we could go back?' In tears, the remnant of groundhogs remembered their bitter lesson in the valley of death. Cause and effect, it's the law of nature designed by the Creator. Negligence will be frowned upon, and accountability will be warranted in due time. 'If only we'd opened our minds to the truth,' croaked another groundhog, limping away into the sunset. 'If-if only.'

"Like the autumn leaf carried along a stream to the sea, the remaining groundhogs' journey pressing forward wasn't without obstacles; some forty summers, it took time and courage for the population to start rebuilding across the river in their new promised land. Of course, groundhogs can't swim," explained Grandma. "How they got across the raging river is another epic story to be told some other time, my searching doves." With a wink, Grandma stretched out her arm for another, well-deserved bowl of moose broth and more wood on the fire.

Back at the House

"**A**nd through all this," I explain to Finn and Diane, "I could communicate with Astor or the guardian angel whenever I wanted. Sitting cross-legged near the fire in the hut, we were glued to the grandmother's story. The whole atmosphere, pre-arranged by the Holy Spirit, was a true blessing. Except for the grandmother's hut, Astor and I lounged the entire two hours on a sofa cloud, observing the people below bustling around the village and across their hunting grounds. By that time, we understood that our presence in the sky or in the hut was in a different period, therefore invisible to them and also harmless.

"So, we stretched our legs and enjoyed our heavenly excursion. By the grace of God, Astor and I were privileged to witness a lifestyle foreign to modern civilization. Our only hope was to remember, and that blessing was granted to us also. I'm happy to say that I returned in one piece from a (once-in-a-lifetime) experience, memory intact, and more to come. It's hard to explain with words. I can't speak for Astor, but for me, at every location where our angel guide brought us, it was like my mind merged into one of their own. I was a tribal family member experiencing the pain and hopes minute by minute in their daily lives. I could somehow walk in their footsteps by simply looking into their eyes. Also, it was as if I'd grown up with the same skills of the wilderness, how to adapt and apply the tools they used at the time. Afterwards, it made me more conscious of people from all walks of life. I am so grateful for our journey. God is good all the time.

"Now, if it's okay with you and Diane, I want to finish my story with another coffee; hold the Bailey's this time, if you please."

"Yes, why not," said Finnegan. "Good timing; the fireplace needs another log."

And Diane added a delightful comment, "More cookies!"

Now off to the next episode for Astor and me—the recent successful hunt in the bustling village.

The Village

Spirits were high in the village due to the fresh kill, a mature bull moose. Food supplies would remain stable for weeks on end. Mother's breast would overflow around the baby's lips, nursing so sweet. Woof! Woof! In their tiny bellies, the multiple vitamins milk overflows. "Take a second to breathe, my feisty bundle," said the attentive mother. She bent her head over the little one spreading a broad smile. "Ouch." Those baby's fingernails are sharp, and the mother discourages the irregular scratching practice by lifting the baby's tiny fist with her pinky. The infant's reflex clenches mommy's finger and won't let go so easily. For new mothers, the babies' needle-sharp teeth piercing their gums while feeding is another family group matter to talk about. The cries of the newborn in the middle of the night thus will decrease, and the mother can at last sleep-sleep.

Tots standing among their clan late in the evening have recovered their cuddling strength and run about. How quick they are on their feet. In a blink, they sidestep here and there periodically to avoid the never-ending ruffling of one's hair by well-meaning family pranksters. A manly bear hug lifts one toddler airborne with mukluks kicking the wind. "Awk! No, Uncle, not again," cried the pleading toddler, "let me down… down." All around, adults laugh out loud at the toddler struggling to free himself, but he is not amused.

A child stands adjacent to his older brother with a hand clutched tight against his stubby torso. A strip of moose meat sticks out from both ends of his tight fist. He leans forward to chew one end for a ravenous, side-mouth bite, always conscious of his older brother's watchful presence looking for mischief. The older one is standing too close and looking too innocent for his liking. In this case, the habit is premeditated; the boy eating the moose strip relaxed his lower lip for the fatty juice to seep out, gravitational style—coagulated drops of moose fat ran down on animal fur clothing covering his chest. In times of plenty, even the very young have a preference—no fat, just meat.

A four-legged, curly-tailed animal, blue and brown eyes following the lad's every move, licks his lips. Why ye of little faith? The half starved dog Runner comes alive again and strolls over for a visit; the moose grease trails an appealing odour. A renewed journey has begun. How refreshing that youngsters can reach out and ruffle Runner's cocky head, its height equal to their own. The dogs that have been quarantined rebound, tongues hanging with pointy ears. When chasing each other over scraps up and down through the village, they cross the line sooner or later and are disciplined by a side foot to skedaddle. Content with their short-lived rebellious outburst, and the fact that they have survived it, the dogs eventually lie down to digest and loaf. Except for the leader of the band, Burly, who keeps at it, wrestling some beastly shoulder bone. The determined dog struggles and shifts to one side and then the other in a death bite. With a stretched-out neck, and ears lowered, the dog purposely drags the dinosaur bone through unsanitary conditions, the native reasoning that "it will build up their strength not to get sick."

Oaf! "Difficult to walk anywhere when your belly is full," one hunter comments while leaning back, patting bloated ribs.

Good idea! Someone has the common sense to wave off the work saying, "The clean-up of pots can wait till tomorrow."

Oh, hold on, Bear-that-Eats needs help. After his initiation into manhood ten years prior, he got the Bear name and never disappointed the village with his calling. The man is thin as a swamp sapling but eats like a bear caught in a smokehouse. His one-of-a-kind thick native skull never learned from the uncultured habit of "eat 'til you blow." Bear-that-Eats lies flat on the ground with clasped hands on his ballooning stomach; tormented, he groans. His two companions of ill repute stand on either side of him, shaking their heads at the sorry excuse moaning for help. They looked at each other with rolling eyes, arms ready.

The prostrated body lying on his back in dire need of assistance manages to plead with an extended arm.

"Let me sleep in the open tonight, Oaf! I can't move."

The old friends of questionable intention mimic his moaning and then announce to each other, "It's going to be one of those nights. This bloated carcass must be pulled inside by the ankles, or he'll freeze to death." With their backs curved, hauling and not paying too much attention to sticks and stones rolling under Bear-that-Eats' loosely bouncing head, they pull him to safety inside the family hut with only minor cuts and bruises.

When leaving, one friend exclaims, "Oh! He gets heavier by the seasons." The other groan in agreement. They leave Bear-that-Eats inside the entrance, lying with arms outstretched on a floor mat, snoring. His relatives will take over from there if they ever wake up.

The Cloud

Astor ordered another bowl of grapes for us, and we shifted outdoors once more with our angel guide stretching out his arm for another episode not far from the village, near the river. There, tragedy was unfolding with a group of natives congregating. Once again, we lounged in our sofa cloud and bore witness, the people below oblivious to the cloud with two people sitting and the angel standing.

To Be Dead

Death-dying-to-be-dead. After the devastating news of her lover, the village people gave the young woman a new name, Lonesome-dove. Call it a senseless accident, a foolish slip over wet stone, a stupid, awkward fall. It happened so suddenly, returning after the hunt, his hunting companions explained, helpless with open arms.

To soothe and say something meaningful, another suggested, "The river took his spirit under the white water and didn't let go?"

Someone turned and scowled at him for his tactless remark.

"Do we rush forward to hold her in our arms, hushing-consoling?" the people thought, but no one dared. Friends stood hopeless, waiting for the young woman to fall apart and die. Lonesome-dove's heart tore out in anger. She spat in a snarl, pierced eyes demanding, "Explain what went wrong. Tell me. Why is my soul mate not coming back?" She moaned. Greybird was fine when he left this morning." A pause, then her eyes grew wide. Reality clued in like a stone lodged inside her heart, and rage drove her in a semi-circle, screaming, "I hate death; I hate it when people die." Lonesome-dove veered backwards. The body of the young woman contorted to a fetal position. She took refuge under a thick, shadowy black spruce, fiercely grieving her lover Grey-bird. In howls, she gripped her stomach with both hands as if pierced by an arrow, but the pain was much worse, so much deeper, to the bone marrow. She cried out again and again in a trailing voice, "I hate death; I hate it when people die." Overwhelmed, Lonesome-dove leaned far to her left side but did not fall over.

It was as if death had propped her against a tree to show off his handiwork, the accuser boasting, "Look, people, I have banished pure love."

Lonesome-dove's jaws clenched the wind, saliva dripping down her chin. Tiny droplets on her forehead turned to blood. Not a time to act civilized. The howling from such a young person was subhuman, not of this earth. It was enough for any stout warrior standing near to shudder and walk away. For two whole winters after this tragedy, the village people wondered, "Lonesome-dove, our Lonesome-dove, will she ever find love again?"

The answer on Lonesome-dove's face was still evident in the budding spring following the third winter. "Leave me alone. I don't believe in love anymore." Or so she thought.

Astor and I contemplated each other in silence after

witnessing Lonesome-dove's calamity, the accidental death of her soul mate, Grey-bird. The incident reminded me of my existence, dealing with loved ones like my father dying. Forgive my personal reference.

Years ago, death had made a mockery of my father, and I hated it too, and I would not forget. I long for the day. I long for that day when our Lord Jesus Christ will come down from heaven, grab hold of this death, and cut it down for good. And by His grace, by the grace of our Father in heaven, I long for the day when we will see this death roll under our feet and rise no more. Glory be to God.

Off to our next episode—the axe-fire plateau. We learned about all sorts of innovative working tools used at the time. Sadly, the prominent device that fascinated me the most had been lost through time, the famous axe-fire structure. Nonetheless, what a treat that was, Astor and I carrying a bowl overflowing with heavenly grapes with our angel guide. Just so you know, throughout the whole trip, for sanitary reasons, Astor was allowed to keep his toothpick.

Axe-Fire Plateau

On the following day in their time, women, young and old, gathered in groups to talk and work at the axe-fire plateau. The levelled granite bedrock was a unique place near the village and spreading into the woods. A place with good elevation, void of vegetation and tree growth. The view overlooked the main river portage trekking by and the porcupine trail that led to Porcupine Lake (natives don't complicate things). The location had a bird's eye view all around for scavengers. Taking a couple of bows and arrows solved the problem of chasing away crows from stretched-out raw hides.

The axe-fire plateau was an important strategic location for the village. By glancing over their shoulders, the villagers could detect anyone passing in and out, travelling to gather wood, pick berries in the summer, hunt, or do other daily activities. Most importantly, a communal rectangular log structure approximately twenty feet by thirty feet and having the height of two people was built at the centre of the bedrock plateau, roof included. The four main corner posts were secured by piles of flat stones circling wide enough to utilize as sitting benches inside the building and out.

This is important, people; I need to elaborate on the curious axe fire at the centre of the lodge. It was an indispensable cutting tool for the village, built up and improved over countless generations and then lost. For starters, the village people designed a square fire pit with a flat stone as thick as a hand and just over knee high with the front left half open at the bottom; they took care to block the higher front half with another well-placed narrow stone. The top edge of the stone box needed to be reasonably flush all around. The team involved in this unique design must have paddled along the river's shore for days to find the other two almost-perfect slabs.

The stones were approximately the same size with a distinct straight edge to one side, large enough to make a flat roof. They then slid the two together on top, leaving a large gap that a person could run his fingers along the centre. They carefully sealed the stone walls inside and out with heat-resistant riverbed clay; yes, the very same clay used for pottery. Then the magic axe-fire cuts began, usually supervised and operated by older children one step from adulthood. In front and below, the firepit's opening was stuffed with kindling to start a vigorous fire that would shoot through the stone slot on the ceiling in a tall, thin orange flame. With sawhorse benches placed to either side at the same height, operators were ready to place long structural poles with the stump still attached or any logs that needed cutting in lengths over the axe flame. Periodically, they rolled the pole a quarter turn at a time for the favoured tapered beaver cut.

In no time, they had a charred, blunt end ready to stick in the ground. Most pole material for framing huts, smoking, and tanning racks was gathered in flat, swampy areas. Like the hair on a dog, the spruce saplings grew tall and bunched together without losing much of their circumference. The soil was poor and drenched all season, so after a growth spurt, they died, standing tall and bone dry. That tough-dry wood texture is especially damaging to flint axes; sparks would fly when attempting to cut those dead saplings. With the soft ground and soaked roots, add air exposure and the bottom rots super-fast.

When the village people came across acres of these trees in swamps, it was not difficult to bend them back and forth, snap the punky roots, and pull the whole tree out. The timber pole came loose, still attached to the stump, its stubby roots broken-star shaped. They trimmed the limbs with a flint axe and snapped the top end at the required diameter with their feet. It was like a production line—some workers tied the saplings a handful at a time on the ground, and others carried out the bundles to the designated dog-sled landing. Remember, black swamp muck rarely froze in winter.

Once hauled to the village on dog sleds, the axe fire took over. This type of village material gathering was best done in late winter, after a thaw followed by a cold spell. The thick icy crust would easily support body weight when the villagers travelled by foot and dog sled. The stumps and top ends cut off by the axe fire were not wasted. The children smashed the roots into chunks and fed them to the axe fire, along with regular firewood.

The name was adapted with the obvious. The controlled orange flame flaring through the narrow gap performed like an axe, cutting accurately and without the endless chopping with a flint axe. The axe fire had saved many flint axes from chipping away to useless in no time and eliminated tedious labour. It was essential for any thriving village to have a good supply of long, thin framing poles for their huts, tanning frames, and smokehouses at the fishing camp. The sturdy spruce poles would last for many summers.

Also, the renowned village spear made of hardwood saplings was cut to size at the axe fire. With the length of a deer running, it was a formidable weapon, perfectly balanced when gripped in the middle, ready to thrust. A broad, razor-sharp flint with a penetrating tear-drop point was inserted at the end. The long spears were used mainly for rare ceremonial hunts and home protection against the bold grey bear and starving packs of wolves. It was usually tucked away overhead inside the hut's entrance so that a family member could run and grab it on their way out. Even an eight-year-old boy or girl could turn into a formidable opponent against any beast with a ten-foot spear pointed at the midsection.

While sitting on our sofa cloud during the axe-fire tour, Astor and I made ourselves at home. Since we both held a bowl of exquisite fruits on our laps, we started throwing grapes at each other. I got Astor on the nose several times; it was an easy target. Heh, we don't think you should blame us for this; the angel started the whole thing. He said not to worry; God's provision overflows all the time. Now, on to our next episode dealing with young people applying themselves for the good of the village.

Next Episode—Springtime

"Time to sharpen your fingers, children; the village axe-fire house needs fixing."
The announcement flashed dark looks on the faces of the youngsters face who had done it before. It was a tedious task inflicting numb fingers with stuffy noses, and after it was all done, the gatherers would have itchy arms. Caught inside the hut, children shifted to walk out, heads downcast and claiming weakness of the knees. The bunch dragged their feet while looking at each other. A drawn-out sigh made it all worthwhile. "How long will this take?" one mumbled. In their minds, it looked like forever.

In a forward stoop, a grandmother fell behind; with her cheerful, boisterous voice, she extended both arms at the front entrance and took charge, the bouncer for *outside you go, children*. Every year, the scheme to argue fatigue failed to work. Walking outside, the chore-bearers knew each other's thoughts. The oldest said, "I want to go into the pine forest with my bow to hunt squirrels."

The other wished to "spear-fish with my

grandfather at the monster lake."

Yet another, "Hunt groundhogs with my dog."

The typical grandfather replied, "Shake it off, short stuff, and let's get it done." Short humans had dropped piles of green, thumb-sized saplings within the hour at the axe-fire house. Some had started repairing the weaving pattern along horizontal sticks that ran feet apart on the outer walls to a man's height, the tight meshing creating wind protection plus shade for hot summers. To some extent, the coarse wooden mesh also prevented night creatures from creeping into nibble hides stretched on poles in various tanning stages. No one could control the wood mice from invading; the rodents were in the open season to stomp or throw sticks at them.

There was also a fair-sized opening under the pitched roof where Astor and I heard the racket. The dark-eyed, egotistical raven could exhibit his presence without qualms. Every second day it seemed, while perched on the top rafter, the raven of the hour ruffled his feathers and croaked as if he owned the whole village. On each visit, the pain in the (you know where) eventually backed down and flew away. That was owed to the individual confronting the annoyance with his bow drawn, aiming the slick arrow at the raven's beak. After the bird's visit grew tiresome, the young, astute hunter muttered an alternative to, "Big mouth, fly away, or I'll shut you up." The raven flew away.

Now, four older children were climbing the walls. Tall elephant grass was for the roof only. Supported by spaced-out pieces of bark covering the framing poles, the rigid, broom-straw-like material was laid on top. The stringy grass was then held together by intertwining spruce roots amid the melee and left sloping down to overhang on the pitched roof. Adding longevity, workers placed lengthy, thin poles on top of the grass, feet apart to press it somewhat flat, thereby steadying the roof from blowing apart in a windstorm.

Clouds gathered, but it was surprising how few drops made it through even in a heavy summer deluge. The dull, putty sound of heavy rain on the cathedral ceiling drew older adults into afternoon power naps. Even after the fleshing knife fell out of their hands, the young didn't bother to rouse the old sleepy heads snoring with their mouths wide open. The storm subsided that evening, with moisture filling the atmosphere. Whisky jacks and chickadees dotted high and low from tree limb to ground level. Even above our cloud, I could detect their tiny wings vibrating in a swoop.

From the daily practice of scraping hides, meat birds could spot discarded bits of animal flesh at a great distance. In a flash, one bird landed before a bitty red dot of pure nutrients. In quick succession, the body twitched sideways to check for incoming thieves. While the nervous head tweaked constantly, it snatched the finger-nail sized morsel lying on the ground quickly enough to perform a disappearing act. "Thank you very much, people," the bird tweaked; down the hatch, it went, and then our frantic guest took off in a burst of feathers. The village's entertainer lands back on the same limb to spy for his next treat, "Chickadee-dee-dee."

Early south winds took care of the river ice. Incoming migration of millions had been activated; below, the ground would shake; above, the sky churned dark with wings, so much so that the horizon disappeared. Always early, the busy-body bumblebee foraged amongst the dandelion flowers, one buzzing hop to another. Along with swollen cheeks, the mommy chipmunks carried mouthfuls of dry grass to disappear headlong into a well-hidden underground burrow, the proud father-to-be nearby, guarding the opening.

What about the inside? Yes, the plateau's village workhouse needed a good spring clean-up appropriately done on hands and knees. With a foot-long log split in half, the people used the edge to scrape loose matter inside the dirt floor to a level smoothness. Don't be a pack rat, they'd say to newcomers; throw out scraps of fur discarded from the winter's mending activities.

In a cloud of dust, a woman stood outside, eyes closed with outstretched arms. Holding a stick in one hand, she swung it back and struck out to beat off the dirt, fleas, and God knows what else the floor mats had accumulated through the winter. Once done, holding a frown, the hard-at-work homemaker pinched both corners of the braided rug, holding it up against the morning sun for inspection. Was it worth keeping for one more summer? This one was still okay for now; the other two? Burn them. Another seasonal task tallied for the year. Using dry elephant grass, the clan braided narrow walking strips reinforced with thin spruce roots, for the icy winter floor. Walking around the hut with thin sleeping moccasins at night, you learned quickly to stay on the mat.

Fresh cedar boughs were hung in bunches along the inside walls for a pleasant spring scent and to discourage insects. He was leaning on a central post of the hut looking out; the young man noticed odd parts of animal bones that had gotten lost in the winter snow but now stuck out, half buried in damp soil outside the entrance. The indifferent individual managed to walk over, pick up the bone, and look for a good opening between trees. The beastly bone was pitched far away with a good arm; an onlooking dog managed to zoom in on the crash site and wandered over to investigate. A pleasant thought came to the young man for the spring season.

Near the village, birch syrup was underway, and not long after, sweet berry picking would wash away the taste of winter meat. On this cool spring morning, all the young and older women had gathered in groups at the axe-fire plateau. The campfire was blazing. They needed to take their sitting positions to find out what was happening around the village and organize priorities. No one dared to disrupt the weekly practice. The atmosphere was bursting with topics to resolve. Occasionally, eyebrows met, drawn to intercede, but who would pick a topic and speak first? There was so much to talk about and so little precious time.

Situations need to be elaborated on and expanded, like elaborating the hunting skills of their men while needle threading in a matter-of-fact way.

Their boisterous Full-moon spoke out first, like umpteen times before. "Ah! My man's backpack," said Full-moon, holding it up. "Look at that, soaked right through to the inside with black muck caked at the bottom. What am I supposed to do with this disaster?" Dripping in the dark, earthy liquid, the pitiful backpack hung from her outstretched arm. Shaking her head in disbelief, she continued. "What needs tossing to teach that absent-minded man of mine?" She didn't wait for an answer; they didn't expect her to. "He simply throws down the pack and walks away; I tripped over the lump outside our entrance this morning and hung it up on the pole where it supposed to be, by then, a waste of my time." The backpack still hung from her closed fist. She tugged it around, hoping to find a dry spot, but there was none.

Sitting across the fire, Tall-bear raised her head to study the dilapidated pack. Both hands were still engrossed in her lap, stripping goose feathers for arrows. Her scowling face evolved quickly in agreement with Full-moon. The backpack did look pitiful. Tall-bear concluded that, with all the work the women put in, the men should be more considerate. Although Tall-bear would never agree outright with Full-moon in public gatherings, after all, they were known to be rivals. Why go spoiling the fun? The conversation grew colourful if you interrupted Full-moon's logic.

The others glanced at each other, for they perceived grey clouds circling. Whoa, Tall-bear took the initiative; contradicting Full-moon, she spoke in defence of the man's hunting habits. After all, he wasn't around to defend himself. Tall-bear made fun of Full-moon's predicament by quoting a child's adventure story. "Oh, that poor little fox out of breath with tail feathers in his mouth," she piped up. "Big-talker would certainly starve without Full-moon's intervention."

Snuffs and concealed laughter spread through the snickering crowd. Another old clan member, Wise-eye, held open hands, depicting a poor fellow begging for substance. The prudent village counsellor rarely spoke out in casual gatherings, let alone participated in jesting others. Her act reared a chorus of jolted laughter, swaying upper bodies, and hand clapping. Whoosh! The floodgates were open. Rushing spontaneous conversation exploded over, under, and sideways. The men knew to stay far away.

"Try to intervene," cautioned a man, "and you may lose an arm." On the sober side of things, people knew how proud and diligent Full-moon was in all her daily tasks. They were grateful, especially in lean times and emergencies. Like one-time last winter. Panic! The family urgently needed ointment from the balsam tree for a severe cut on a child's arm. Stepping out in the middle of the night in deep snow to gather ointment in the forest was not trivial. Wait, Full-moon made extra last summer with rolls of clean deer hide strips for binding. Phew! Let's ask her for some.

Several of her relatives made occasional remarks like, "Even in late spring, you won't find a speck of mould or dog hair on Full-moon's dried berries."

Full-moon oversaw quality control when food needed to be stored and preserved for winter consumption. She proudly announced, "I don't like to see anyone pulling dog hair between their teeth when eating winter meat at our gatherings, or scraping off green mould, for that matter. Bear fat is not an ointment; use it lavishly and pay attention to your wrapping; be vigilant," she would fuss about in a governess's voice. Focus.

Now Full-moon spoke what was really on her mind. Here we go. "I heard Silver-tail say that killing that large bull moose took many arrows. When I picked up Big-talker's backpack this morning, I noticed four arrows missing from his quiver pouch."

Tall bear's basket of striped goose feathers was gathering momentum. The tall, dark-haired beauty raised her head, revealing large black eyes fixed in silence. She sat plumb, cross-legged facing the old neighbouring rival, Full-moon. Her black, shiny hair was parted over the shoulders to fall freely in front. Her full lips held a smile, but the eyes betrayed the true nature of her kindness. Astor and I noticed immediately that the delicate deerskin blouse she wore breathed supreme craftsmanship—skillfully tailored and decorated with an intricate porcupine quill pattern depicting a legendary encounter with a bear.

Tall-bear loosened her hands and relaxed the fingers pinching goose feathers, and then she leaned back unconcerned, speaking casually. "You may want to look inside Big-talker's backpack, Full-moon," she said.

Feeling agitated and suspicious, Full-moon replied swiftly, "Why? What for?" Oops! Full-moon felt regret as soon as the words came out, but it was too late. Depicting a sour face, Full-moon bit her lip in anguish; the rabbit trap had sprung.

Tall-bear replied. "Well, you might find four dead squirrels inside." In cahoots with Tall-bear, a roar of laughter rippled across the floor. Squat bodies rocked back and forth. A needle had pricked a joker's finger; in pain, she cupped her hand and sucked the tip mournfully.

Full-moon witnessed the incident and yelled over people's heads, "Serves you right for laughing."

That reprisal made matters worse. Some leaned to one side with their arm extended to slap and ruffle the closest sitting bodies. At that moment, Full-moon scowled and thought, "I despise what's all around me."

A hand tugged at Full-moon's shoulder as comrades do in the hour of battle. "We're all in this together."

Heads shake yes-yes, and slowly regular breathing resumed. The joker lamented again, "The point of my needle broke off in my finger, ouch!" More laughter. In the past, Full-moon would have lashed out with certainty at Tall-bear, but not this time. She caught herself, and no one saw her body twitching forward to lunge. She only glared at Tall-bear, fuming. Then, deciding to respond secretively, she gradually closed her fist around a pile of dirt on the floor and flung a handful at her foe. Dust and debris flew toward Tall Bear's face. The attempt proved feeble; the light sticks choked with dust scattered harmlessly halfway to her tormenter. Although, the message was clear; Full-moon was not amused.

More smothered chuckles spilled out among the troop, although this time only from a few brave souls. Even so, it proved difficult to hold a grudge against Tall-bear. Look at that chirping face with a broad smile, thought Full-moon, with those large eyes smirking. Youth born clever and playful with a touch of cruelty, but it was hard to stay angry at a princess that winked at you.

But make no mistake, if she continued quarrelling with Tall-bear, more trickery would spill out like spring water. This time, Full-moon did not strike back at her blood relative, Tall-bear. She was proud of herself for reacting calmly, even though every fibre in her body told her to retaliate. Then, the storm passed. For no reason in particular, the group drew silent and resumed their daily tasks for a whole two minutes.

Two minutes of silence was a rarity for mothers congregating at the village axe fire.

The Legend of Full-moon

A precious child was born, and her father named her Full-moon in response to her round face and huge, bright eyes. To seal all arguments, the baby girl was born in the fall during a full moon. Growing up as a young teenager had its challenges. For a time, some of the boys in the village, like partners in crime, came around to stir trouble. They challenged each other to see who would be the first to do it. The young empty heads pranced about, mocking Full-moon's birth identity that her father had proudly chosen. Just for laughs, one suggested that her name, Full-moon, was the result of her large breasts. With both hands cupped to their chests, the troublesome boys pranced around, imitating the burden of bearing a cumbersome load in front of her while walking. Of course, they were always cautious, performing their demeaning jests at a safe distance; they'd laughed out loud at her expense as the boys dared each other to prance around.

Humiliated, Full-moon boiled with anger and chased after them with no concept of personal injuries.

But they were all so agile and nimble on their feet—poof! Like a bunch of jackrabbits, they simply scattered in the woods, nowhere to be seen. Until one day, that one faithful day, when the tide turned in her favour.

From the corner of her eye, Full-moon noticed that the runny nosed Big-talker had gotten distracted in his rivalry towards her and wasn't paying attention. After snatching a walking stick along the way and running toward him, Full-moon caught-up after Big-talker tripped over a root and fell headlong. Guess what? His buddies in crime took off, leaving him stranded on the ground. Out of breath and filled with anger, she stood over Big-talker, who laid prostrate in the dirt. While raising her walking stick high up into the sun, she screamed blue murder.

The fishing camp stood nearby at the river's edge. A handful of villagers fussing about the campsite were busy tying up fish racks and stuff. They heard the commotion and rose from sitting positions to look at each other, puzzled. They gazed to where the odd howling had originated from in the woods. Big-talker's punishment echoed across the river-valley as far out as the eagle's nest. Needless to say, the Big-talker gang didn't come around after that. And it came to pass that Full-moon became a warrior.

The Legend of Tall-bear

As for Tall-bear, her childhood was not quite ordinary. Tall-bear stood over six feet, which was extremely tall for a native girl, and that needed a thorough explanation, leaving no stone unturned. The story was told and retold at campfires for centuries about the little girl who, at the tender age of five summers, was re-named Tall-bear.

One sunny day in mid-summer, when Tall-bear was a toddler, her mother, like usual, went out early that morning to pick blueberries on the hillside near the village. Filled with the enthusiasm of the innocent, naturally the little tot trekked along with button elbows holding a beaver grass basket that spanned beyond her body. The berries were plentiful that year, an underbrush forest exploding in blue that could satisfy mother bear and her three cubs by evening. The thin branches curved loaded to ground level with handfuls of sweet fruit begging to be eaten. When standing on higher ground, you'd think that Mother nature had rolled out a welcoming blue carpet for all to walk on.

No one was to blame for what happened; once

crouched, a mother's mind wanders when therapeutic sun rays commence to soothe stiff shoulder blades. As her mother rose from time to time, walking over to the next patch of blue, a lukewarm breeze relieved her hot cheeks. How could a mother not grow lax, even forgetful, of a child?

On this particular summer day, her mother remained determined with the crucial project—to dry and store sweet fruits for her family so as to face another long winter ahead. Within calling distance and bent from the waist, the energetic homemaker embraced low bushes with incredible picking skills. With supple fingers and hands that moved like a cat, mother filled her deep basket with tons of berries.

Heavens! Mom didn't notice her little girl wandering off on her own, even though the little princess had been severely instructed to sit, eat her lunch, and nap under the shaded spruce tree with the other full basket. "Mother won't be far," were her last words, other than a promise to "be back soon." What part of that didn't the little girl understand? Mercy me.

The mother went on picking, in her own little world, oblivious to her daughter's whereabouts. Grasping the oversize basket with both hands, the little munchkin skipped away, mindless. "Let's play the butterfly chase," she decided on a whim. Running, more like hopping, her zigzagging through blueberry patches brought to mind the story of Little Red Riding Hood. She hop-chased the yellow winged wonder, her chubby hand rising skyward and waving stop-stop, as she held her basket at the waist with the other. Ah! She giggled, surmising, "That sun-butterfly is quick to leap on colourful wings, and he's teasing me to run faster."

On that blustery day, at every hop over fallen trees, her long, black hair trailing horizontal, the chase was on. "Maybe the butterfly is inviting me to his house," she thought. I don't know where little girls get those funny ideas either. As birds chirped in the woods, a flock of yellow butterflies coaxed the stout, two-legged girl with her disproportionately large basket through blueberry patches; they coaxed her over the hill farther out. They coaxed, come-on, come-on.

Then, for some inexplicable reason, the sun-butterflies disappeared, and a large black bird appeared, unannounced. The solitary raven made his royal presence perched on top of a tall black spruce. To say the least, his croaks were abrasive, and he couldn't carry a tune if his life depended on it. The knuckleheaded raven flew from one treetop to the other, drawing the innocent little one farther and farther away, to the point where no person from the village, let alone her mother, could detect her pleading calls for help. The conspirator ruffled his feathers from head to tail as if to wash away responsibility. His jutting beak dipped high and low like he was laughing, having fun. If the beak had lips, his would surely have curved up in a crooked smile. While perched high up in the trees, instead of helping, the trouble-maker raven took pleasure in the little girl's predicament. A catastrophic event was about to unfold, and he sat there watching with cruel, devious intent.

Maybe a large tree once fell on his head. No one knew what was wrong with the raven.

Regardless, a little girl's worst nightmare was now unfolding in front of us, thirty yards above on a sofa-cloud. We couldn't scream for help. We couldn't warn the victim or throw a stick at the knucklehead raven. All Astor and I could do was observe. I remembered reciting over and over in my head: you are staring at the past; it has already happened. God is in control. But that didn't help much. I ground my teeth in anger. Disgusted, Astor was pitching grapes at the raven. A heartfelt gesture, but it didn't do much either.

Let's go back to our forgetful little girl all alone and lost in the woods.

Yards away from the little blueberry picker, a shadowy figure emerged. An old bear stood on his back legs, his front paws out like a dog begging for snacks. Surprised, the old black bear with blue lips belched and peered down at the child, wondering, "What's that tiny creature doing in my woods?" He snorted. "Picking my blueberries, I see. How odd, having long black hair on top of her head like that blowing in the wind while running on two legs; how fragile she looks, holding her basket waist high half filled with my blueberries.

Question: what do big black bears do when stuffed with blueberries and bored to smithereens? Answer: They look for trouble and amuse themselves, that's what. The furry ears swivelled back and forth in all direction, listening to detect whether the little girl was alone, and yes, she was all alone. Excellent. "I have time to spare," he thought with a grunt. "Hold on, as a precaution, I will check far away," said the old, cautious one. The bear swung his long neck over to one side and then the other, his mouth dripping white foam. While exercising a huff and more huffs, his wet, rubbery nose flared for maximum scent intake. Sniff-sniff, nothing? For miles around, the flea-infested bear and one little girl were definitely alone in the forest.

"Hmm, how sweet," murmured the bear. "The thought of a little one alone crying almost draws a tear into my left eye." Without warning, the old stinky bear went down on all fours and started chasing the little girl through the forest.

The toddler cried out, "Mommy! Mommy, where are you?"

"Your mother is preoccupied, my precious. But you keep running," said her guardian angel. "Hide in a cave if you can; for today, in the valley of death, Mother cannot help you," explained the lady angel. "So, run-run."

Ah! So horrifying to watch. The little one tried to run away as best she could, but her short legs soon stumbled over blueberry shrubs, and she tumbled headlong into the bushes. Terrified, the toddler burst out crying, her tears smearing with dirt on her cheeks. Misery! The shiny black hair soon got tangled up with mud, thistles, and sticks. Her throat felt raw from screaming. "What a mess I'm in," she blurted out, sobbing.

The goofy bear was enjoying himself thoroughly,

saying, "The girl is so easy to chase, and I delight to watch her fall." The insensitive beast made fun of her short status. He took pleasure in her struggles in attempting to run away from her nightmare. The fleabag grew relentless in his foolish game of spreading fear on the helpless little one, hiding behind a stump, then a rock, and then loping to catch up to her short bum running away. He did it with a certain amount of agility for an old bear, not to mention a wheelbarrow full of glee.

It seemed at the time a fun game to play; the bear yahooed, laughing at her expense. This was what the pea-brained bear dished out at that moment, without thought of any consequences for the future. Like the old farmers used to say, "Chicken today, feathers tomorrow." Far out in the forest valley, a child's voice cried out bitterly; with all the wind those tiny lungs could take, she cried out and cried out for help. Being taken so far away from her mother by that irresponsible raven hadn't helped matters. Her pleading to be rescued was doomed from the start.

Her guardian angel said, "Run-run-run, for now, help is on its way." Although, with her short legs, she simply couldn't get away fast enough. Heavens! To make matters worse, the handle on her basket tore, and all the berries she'd worked so hard for scattered on the ground, lost forever. The young girl stopped and looked down at her withered basket and got angry at herself; she knew better. How many times had mother explained? How many times had Grandpa cautioned her to "Stay close to your mother, don't wander, and watch out for the bears." How could she be so careless and forgetful?

"What's the raven's problem anyway?" said the frustrated little girl. "We feed him all the time at the village. Papa said the raven is a guardian to our people and a friend. I thought for certain that his directions would take me back to Mother. Right now, I hope he chokes on a rotten carcass." The distraught girl frowned." I hate that pesky raven. I hate him-I hate him."

Above heavy treetops loaded with pinecones, the majestic eagle soared in the wind, just below the clouds. Even though his talons trailed loose, he still looked menacing and a tad deadly. The eagle's hooked beak traversed from side to side, on the look-out for prey. From rabbits to a yearling fawn, they were no match for the king eagle, so run and hide, you warm-blooded creatures. To activate possible miss-steps or panic when closing in on his prey, ear-piercing screeches resonated across the land. Stealth, silence, and surprise were the keys to a successful hunt. "Oh, but wait, what's that noise?" thought the eagle. "What's going on down in the valley?"

The piercing eye of the eagle pinpointed the disturbance around the blueberry shrubs half a mile below. A black oval blob was chasing a tiny toddler with flailing arms. "How peculiar," the eagle thought. Oaf! It had been a slow, uninteresting morning for the meat hunter. Puzzled and somewhat curious, the raptor decided to take a closer look. To dip downward, the elongated feathers parted like fingers and curled upward from the accelerated wind current applied under the wing. From the ground, a large, shadowy cross would whoosh overhead in a semi-circle; no doubt, the human eye would struggle just to keep on top of the eagle's path as he swooped above.

Like a wind tunnel, the body mass of feathers exploded in each and every way and went vertical in the air, braking fast. Legs extended with talons expanding large enough to engulf a human face. This time, the talons functioned as landing gear clamping down on a treetop. The king of the sky perched at the very tip of an old spruce specimen, staring at the bear below. With one wing half open for balance, the eagle had this displeased hunch about him, with penetrating yellow eyes to match. The eagle's massive volume flexed the treetop that arced like a bow, thus balancing the eagle's massive body perched on two legs.

The sturdy tree trunk vibrated all the way down to its roots and held less a dozen pinecones. The eagle's head scooped low and flat, penetrating yellow eyes piercing under shadowy eyebrows. Bobbing high and low to the chest cavity, the eagle let out piercing cries at the bear. At about twenty times the volume of blackboard screeching, the eagle's hooked beak parted, his abrasive tongue sticking out in the centre like a spear ready to jab. Without ceasing, the royal presence scolded the bear for being so cruel to the little girl, raking the old fellow up and down one side and then the other like there was no tomorrow.

The bear felt as if he was being trampled by an avalanche and all that was left was to die. "Heavens," the eagle screamed, "why are you making chase to such a fragile creature that has done nothing to you? The forest is full of berries for anyone's fancy."

The black mass of fur, poised like a stump, stared at the treetop in dumb silence, clearly humiliated. His lips fell in a flipped 'U' shape. Not a proud moment for our pathetic bear. The wide-eyed loser stood like a pillar of salt. It looked like brother bear had gotten egg on his face and was still trying to declare innocence with his fused expression. Then, great remorse bellowed in his big, goofy heart. The humongous fur animal slid low, scraping his paws against the ground as though attempting to disappear. As his ears fell subdued between the blueberry stems, his lower jaw pushed dirt forward into a small pile over his rubbery nose. The front legs stretched out on each side, making even bigger piles of dirt over his massive claws. In a childish attempt to be invisible, the daunting creature bent one paw inward over his grey muzzle to cover his eyes. With the bear's flanks heaving on that hot summer day, I heard grumbling emerge from the pit of his stomach. Gradually, white foam bubbled between relaxed lips. The air turned foul. Out of despair, he shut his eyes to hide in black. The bear thought, "I want to disappear and die." As the old creature babbled emotions like ocean swales in a hurricane, finally a tiny beam of kindness penetrated his thick skull. A spirited solution entered to calm the troubled waters. Alas! The ship-wrecked bear would reach the shoreline and live another day. The bear wanted to redeem himself.

The disheartened father-time bear rose and spoke to the eagle these cleansing words: "I regret bitterly what I have done and confess that my conduct is inexcusable. Give me time to make amends to the little girl." The aged bear blurted out his thinking while sitting on his rump with front paws flaring in front like a human praying. The bear continued earnestly, for fear of interruption. "Before winter arrives, I will call out to the roots of the forest on her behalf for the little girl's misfortune. I will intervene earnestly and ask for the reddish roots to release her precious oil that stirs growth."

By that time, the pious bear was actually crawling on his belly, searching for roots to demonstrate his willingness to act accordingly. The scene looked pitiful. Then the bear sat up with one paw stretched to the sky, poking his rounded claw like an index finger and pointing to the sky. "Along the tiny girl's path going home from picking berries would present the best opportunity for a child's bare feet." The bear lowered its massive paw. "She will eventually walk on top of the prickly moss loaded with tiny white sacs."

The heavenly liquid contained oils for bears and people to grow like giants in physical form. "Millennium ages prior, from jack-rabbit size, that was how our brother grizzly bear grew and grew," the bear reminded the eagle. "As for the girl, at every step for a whole summer, the green moss will secrete golden liquid between her toes. In time, the oil-saturated skin will sprint the little girl's growth so that never again will she stumble over blueberry patches. And, when a fully grown woman, she will be as tall as a bear standing on his hind legs."

A moment of silence fell among the two, the eagle scowling and the bear hoping, waiting. Tick-tock, tick-tock… and then? After considering, the eagle was pleased with the bear's plan, and they made it so.

In summers that turned whiskers white on the snout of a deer, Tall-bear grew and grew. All the while, she retained her mother's elegance. The young woman's muscular curves were well proportioned and pleasing while in motion; her long, black hair with dark, penetrating eyes drew young men travelling by canoe record distances. Arriving close together (the ones paddling), many stared at their feet while scraping dirt with no words to speak. With one exception: the wiry Lone-grey-wolf.

The word *grey* was not in association with age. On the contrary, the young man had five winters less than Tall-bear. Curiously, he'd been born with a permanent streak of grey hair on one side of his head. So, after his enduring paddling excursions, the name came naturally to the village, Lone-grey-wolf.

The royal beauty, Tall-bear, was a true artist when it came to beads. After the hunt, bracelets and necklaces were her passion in quiet times. The most elaborate necklaces were created by her mother and were Tall-bear's most cherished possessions. She carried the fine, interlocking stones with nobility. Tiny beads of bright orange seashells and pliable yellow stones to add weight complemented each other in delicate strand patterns that had no end. The tall, attractive girl looped the necklace twice around her neck, with one strand arcing lower. Hidden behind thick, braided hair, her golden beads traced over firm shoulders to hang free in front, thus capturing dignity on refined deer skin.

The Legend of Wise-eye

Wise-eye, the oldest and grandmother of the largest clan, sat beside Full-moon. Like I mentioned before, she rarely participated when acquaintances talked ill of people, even in a light-hearted manner. The best that a person could get out of Wise-eye was her secretive smile. The time has come when I need to explain how her name, Wise-eye, came about. If I didn't, it wouldn't be fair to the others.

This happened long ago; it was rumored that, on one cold winter night, her mother had a difficult delivery. That caused a nerve in the baby's right eye to bruise and detach itself. As a result, the eyelid went limp and drooped down to her cheek, giving the impression that her face was pondering life with one eye half closed. Also, an old aunt concluded that, to make things a bit worrisome, the girl's features were plain to look at. But her father saw none of it.

On the second summer after the little girl's first steps, something needed to change. The father warrior went for a long walk alone, staring at the distant full moon and composing a lullaby about his daughter's unique birthmark. While singing his song, the name *Wise-eye* felt well suited for her. After all, her name would be spoken out loud time and time again through the seasons. "Wise-eye-Wise-eye." The girl would have no choice but to accept her calling and grow in wisdom. "Either way, no one will mock my bundle of joy," said the astute warrior. "If they do, before I fall, many of my arrows will find their mark on the mockers."

And so it came to pass; Wise-eye grew up to be the oldest and wisest of them all. Most of the time, she appeared unaware of her birthmark and happy as could be while flourishing to adulthood. The warrior's warning was seared on the villagers' forehead. No one dared to tease her about the eye.

Now Wise-eye leaned slightly to one side, brushing Full-moon with her silver, braided strands of hair. She conversed in a soft voice, stretching out her fingers as if holding a moment in time. She reached to touch Full-moon's forearm. "How are things coming along with your man's new hunting pack?"

Sitting cross-legged, Full-moon's shoulders drooped, and she shook her head. Not so good. Frustrated, she announced as if defeated, "Oaf! I hope this one last longer than one summer. No matter what I do, in no time at all my best leather turns to shreds on that man's back. You'd think I'd been using spider webs for stitching and no glue."

Wise-eye remembered the early years of back-pack sewing. Within the first handful of winters, stitching was a skill achieved by trial and error and perseverance.

A rendezvous of the young and old seamstresses was critical; it was like gathering priceless pearls at the bottom of a deep, silted ocean—it took teamwork, one above, the other below. Wise-eye whispered, "Now there, don't get discouraged, my hopping mother of five little ones." Reduced to skin and ligaments, her fragile hand reached out. With her arm parting the heavy shoulder blanket, Wise-eye finger-rubbed the sturdy leather of Full-moon's backpack.

By the closeness of the old woman, shivers from being cared for, radiated up her right side. Full-moon's heart yielded to Wise-eye's counsel; her shoulders relaxed in a tingling sensation. What to do now?

Lavishing tenderness, the patriarch spoke in a low voice with a hint of reproach, thus clarifying the methods of the durable stitching practices. "Let's organize this pile a bit better so we can see."

Full-moon relaxed the hand that held the hunting pack, which had gone flat from her arm resting on top. Gazing forward, she resigned herself to be taught a more excellent way. The old woman gingerly pulled the unfinished sack towards her and immediately scrutinized the stitching by flopping the backpack from one side to the other. Her adroit index finger traced the seams stitched by Full-moon. She bit her lower lip, hinting, *there is hope.* Hope expressed in a soft, nasal huff.

Wise-eye finally made the long-awaited head movement, "Yes-yes, very good." Her uninterrupted finger movement continued around and up the shoulder strap. Like a schoolteacher commencing her class, Wise-eye propped back her shoulders to dish out precise instruction. "You double-stitched the side together, that's thoughtful," she said. "Now go back under with a narrow strip on the inside. See? Like this."

She shot a quick glance at Full-moon to see if she was following. "And don't forget the bow curves to accommodate the shape of a man's shoulders; a hand's width by a forearm's length is a reasonable allowance for a comfortable body fit. That way, the pack will cling to Big-talker's body more naturally, and therefore there will be less chance of it getting caught while hunching through thick underbrush. For the outside, on your last turn don't forget the red shells. Make it pleasing to the eye by spacing them out with the width of your thumb first, then the middle finger followed by the small finger and do repeats. Tuts! When it comes to porcupine quills, you inherited the magic hands from your grandmother."

Stretching out her arms, Wise-eye pinched the pack from the top corners. A renowned homemaker imagining how it would look once completed. With tilted, prickly eyes, a wide smile grew on Wise-eye's face and, if you could imagine, more wrinkles. She exclaimed in a hoot! "Oh yes, your man of thunder, Big-talker, will carry himself handsomely when travelling with his clan."

A broad smile transported to Full-moon's face. She couldn't wait to finish her backpack.

The crisp call of a blue jay resonated in the forest as

the busy people beneath us, sat content. On our cloud, from a distance, Astor and I witnessed cross-legged bodies leaning every which way laughing; one bent forward, pointing at the famous backpack, a comment was flung out with little thought, and more laughter exploded. On bright sunny days with plenty, cares were few, the pangs of winter had vanished. The community fire roared in the centre. It was a good day to be alive. Telling stories among friends around a campfire; what more did people need in life?

From the height where a crow flies like a dot, a sea of forest green rolled by, until an eastern mountain range fenced them in like a herd of sheep. They were accompanied by troubling clouds overhead. In all direction, the treeline appeared turquoise. Through the night, near the village, a porcupine had stripped the green bark of a deciduous tree from top to bottom. Astor nudged me in the arm and pointed out how, in contrast to its surroundings, the tree trunk stood ghostly white. During the day, the leisurely specimen rested high, out of sight below the neighbouring giant spruce. Content, with no doubts or worries of detection or being disturbed. Like stars in our firmament, poplar trees by the thousands stood, spaced feet apart. The passive, prickly bark eater slept among them, Wolves and coyotes could circle the giant spruce and yap all they wanted; the porcupine sat, resting high, slightly annoyed by the fuss. His substance for survival was at hand, one living tree away. It must be frustrating at times, to be born carnivore, not capable of partaking in trees that sustain life.

Back to Wise-eye for one last thing, and then we're done.

Wise-eye lowered her voice to speak in secret. Viewing her intent and out of respect for privacy, the others turned their attention away from Wise-eye and Full-moon. The women went about talking among themselves of common things like the work of the day and what was expected for the seasons preserve in trade. Now Wise-eye spoke, inching close to the ear of Full-moon. With a cupped hand, she shaded her lips and whispered, "Consider this, my joy. On the morning that your man Big-talker leaves for the hunt, ask him to wait a minute. Pretend you're fussing over the shoulder fitting of his new pack and look closely into his eyes before speaking. And then, say something like this…

"You're a great provider, sweet man of mine. Try not to rip this pack to shreds if you can. And don't worry about our village axe-fire; the poles will get cut up, flint knives and scrapers will be sharpened, with the fleshing mats spread out ready for you. I'll send the girls to stock up on firewood as we wait for your return." Wise-eye shifted lightly to lean back, contemplating, before swinging an open arm to introduce the sky so to prophesy. "Now step back and observe Big-talker's shoulders rise to the challenge. Remark carefully, the eyes resolving to achieve. Notice the sole of his mukluks when your man walks away. I can promise you this, my joy; his mukluks will hardly be touching the ground. The young men of our village are admirable hunters, although we are the ones who spin them into thunder-bolt-hunters." The aged eyes blinked in a prison of wrinkles. In a flash, her bright smile widened far. Her woody index finger appeared to point discretely at heaven. The other one lifted to shush Full-moon, her narrow lips crimping.

Wise-eye spoke again in a haunted voice. "What I have just declared to you is not meant for men to know. These precious abilities, my joy, are given to us by the great Spirit. We carry them to our graves. Not a word."

At the campfire, after experiencing the heartfelt relations among the village people, Astor and I were taken up in the air above the tree line once more. While we sat on our sofa-cloud, the angel's arms opened wide as if he had wings to fly. The somber-faced angel turned to us and spoke. "Now gentlemen, you will travel into the raven's heart so as to understand his twisted ways and stay clear whenever possible. Not a bad idea, Astor and I thought at the time. After all, a world-renowned French general had said the same thing, "Know your enemies."

Although I don't believe he ever mentioned anything about loving your enemies.

The Raven

High above, from a raven's perspective, the village looked like a smear on white snow. Even so, out of curiosity more than hunger, the urge to investigate prevailed. The raven's stiff feathers arced upward, fanning as one wing dipped, rushing a wide, downward circle. By familiarity more than instinct, the raven knew where to perch at a safe, observatory distance. Over there, the land rose to an outcrop of poplar, a century-old stand of timber clinging to half its living limbs.

Once perched, the raven had a panoramic view of the village. Whoosh! With little room for error, the raven landed expertly on a sturdy limb high above ground. The surface was worn down by other landings —by talons and beaks scraping for the occasional meal, leaving dark bloodstains embedded in the fibre of the wood. The acidic ejection of body waste that had missed the mark enforced the already poor housekeeping. The century-old treetop perch governed a wide view of incoming flight traffic, which might need to be dealt with.

"Here I am, entertain me, I'm bored," the pompous king raven thinks to himself. Soon the urge can no longer be contained. The royal beak parts to voice an enormous croak, followed by two more. Oops! Now his position has been revealed to other birds for miles around. One flits closer. "Never mind, you feeble-minded one," the raven retorted with his enormous ego. The announcement was intentional, designed to instil fear in the other peasant bird. The raven's vocals were distinct and gruff, "My croak is bigger than yours, stand clear."

The revolving membrane applies eye moisture to help the raven focus on land movements coupled with a keen sense of smell. With a King Henry's appetite, his stomach could process anything fresh or half rotten. It all goes down the hatch with a smack of his beak. From past encounters, the raven knew far too well the wonderful opportunities in a congress of two-legged creatures. According to the observant raven, newborns are hatched throughout the seasons inside their huts and later walk outside with no parental supervision. From the animal kingdom point of view, that would not be a wise practice to adopt. They rarely squabbled over food and emerged looking like their parents but shorter. No wait, there was one major difference. The little two-legged people were forgetful, even careless at times, and easy to fool. Any raven could fly over and land in front of them and then hop ahead, pretending to have a broken wing. When they were lured far enough away from the taller ones, the raven could swiftly fly a half circle behind and steal food left beside a stump or hung on low branches.

Ravens could perform the same ruse over and over, and stubby two-legged humans never caught on. Instead of retaliating to get their food back, the little people stood with their arms raised and laughed. Being that thick-headed, (the raven thought) it was surprising so many were still alive and not starving to death.

Let's see, what's on the menu today? A morsel, a bone, a burnt strip of meat tossed on white snow; an easy meal begging to slide inside my royal gullet, the raven concluded. The shiny black head pivoted non-stop with such a glare it was difficult to tell if mister big bird was freaking out or what. Only time and patience were required. His look-out was ideal to sunbathe old bony wings, and the raven waited patiently for dawn.

Lit afar by moonlight, stands of poplar spread out over rolling hills. The cone canopies with their prickly edged barbs beneath the sky painted mauve. Farther north, the boreal forest was tucked knee deep in immense, frozen stretches of white. Appearing angelic, the commanding view summoned the human heart to purity. Perched in the center of all, the pompous king raven dwelled, large and black.

The very next day, which was in the blink of an eye for Astor and me, we sat on our sofa-cloud pointing to the east, trying to distinguish the rackety calls of ravens. The commotion presented an omen for the villagers—a sizable herbivore had given up the ghost. Like a fallen meteor, from a bird's eye view, the black lump trailed red in the snow. Scavengers arrived but kept a respectable distance high above the surrounding trees. No hurry, the fallen beast would not budge. By proper order, they bided their time and patiently waited.

After the village people hit the trail with heavy backpacks and left the killing site, only then would the posse swoop down from the trees screeching hellfire. With fewer kills, it had been a hard winter for the scavengers. Even bits of flesh on fur or blood-saturated snow could make the difference between nesting in the spring for the next generation or not making it through the winter.

While considering the raven's every day life, Astor and I realized that even the large and black have their own cross to bear.

Back Over to the Village

stor and I found ourselves lifted in the spirit and transported back to the village. Hunched over while sitting on blankets near their huts, a dozen people were preoccupied with their task at hand; two campfires were visible. The reddish sun wrapped itself in purple clouds, ready for bed. At a distance, approaching westward, the villagers detected trailing laughter that revealed shortness of breath. A few heads turned at the disturbance, and then all halted their work to see what was happening way out there.

With open mouths, the villagers glanced at each other puzzled. Hands loosened and elbows eased for a moment. The group's collectiveness evaporated quickly. As though they had just discovered a dog hair in their soup, scowls covered their faces. The older generation held the vote for the proper conduct so as not waste any time. At the present, the younger generation was not complying at all. They were running around in the deep snow, which was foolhardy and a waste of energy. (Although the older folks wouldn't admit it, they longed to have such spunk and do the same.)

Under her sky roof, protected by walls on three sides, Wise-eye sat watchful, leaning against her rolled-up Dall sheep blanket. Inside her booth, animal figurines with dream catchers hung on strings, swaying loosely in the breeze. The structure faced the well-travelled Porcupine Trail; one shrewd old woman was open for business and ready to trade. Now, peering in the same direction where the extravagant laughing was taking place, she could not have stretched her neck any longer with her nose in the lead. With pursed lips, she searched on either side for information, but friends were sitting too far away. So, Wise-eye resigned herself to whispering, "What's going on down there?"

This was what was going on down there. After a distracted young man bragged endlessly about his last hunt, some free-spirited girl stole a perfect strip of smoked moose meat right out from under his nose; "That should teach him not to boast," she thought, taking off. The nerve! The indignity!

Appalled, the distraught male crossed his arms, huffing and stomping the snow like a child, screaming, "Stop-stop, you thief. Don't girls know it's a sacrilege to steal smoked meat from men?" The chase for retribution was on.

He growled a warning while running after her, but she knew him well. "My tiger with no teeth." That didn't change anything; the long-legged female was in perfect form and headstrong enough to get away with it. As she ran at full strides in leaps and bounds, her mouth opened wide, showing white teeth chomping the tasty strip of smoke meat. Alas! There was no justice in this world. She was pleased with herself and grew confident in her getaway. "By running fast, I can create a safe distance and finish eating this delightful treat."

But men didn't give up that easily when it came to smoked meat; we would not be cajoled. Pride of ownership and youthful lungs were on his side. Detecting a girly shadow moving fast behind tree trunks, he made the decision to cut across knee-deep snow and get his prize back.

Defying logic, the slim beauty-bandit leaned behind a scrawny tree trunk, giggling. To discern the whereabouts of her disgruntled pursuer, while leaning against the tree, she pressed her cheeks against the rough bark and peeked around the trunk. Chewing with gusto and still in a playful mood, the breathless angel face radiated desire. Then, in a flash, her dark eyes blinked. "It's too quiet. Too normal." She shrugged and wolfed down another bite, moose grease running down her chin.

Woof! A whirlwind sprayed snow drops behind the thief. With a growl, hands interlocked to bear hug the astonished girl. The arms of the young buck wrapping under her ribcage felt like tree trunks. She barely had time to support her upper body. Eyes bulging with panic, she palmed his forearms to strengthen her elbows. Her shoulders tensed to her ears. Uh-oh! Her ribcage flexed; the youthful brute didn't know his own strength. To the young fellow, she was a thieving weasel now airborne, legs thrashing wind, staring at the stars.

Who's the man now? Who the man?

A sudden burst of exploding energy made her spit out some of the tasty smoked meat, and she wailed bloody murder. So that's what was going on down there. The cries of playful, spirited youngsters echoed through the forest.

High above a tree, the raven ruffled his feathers, contemplating escape, but then changed his mind. The miser's eyeballs zeroed in on the tiny bits of smoked meat shooting across the white snow; it would be a shame to leave those to the rodents. Let's wait and see.

Just over the next hill, the silver fox wasn't taking any chances. There was too much tramping of large creatures and strange howling. The four-legged ball of fur trotted back to his den, thinking, "What is going on down there?"

Back to the howling thief. "How is it possible to travel in deep snow so fast?" she thought. "I had a good lead on the guy." It was foolish to struggle with a tiger, even if he was clawless with no teeth. They reached a compromise—the strip of stolen moose meat would be shared. While sensing solid ground under her feet, the bear grip loosened, and she could breathe again. Now she was able to turn and face her only love. Even acting distracted while stepping back to scratch his back against a birch tree, the wiry hunter of many portages deserved his share. She rolled her eyes. "The man is clueless. Might as well take the initiative." She moved forward.

They embraced, seemingly to fight the cold and

search secrets of the heart. The heavy breathing from the chase calmed itself as she cuddled with her lover. In that hour, no one existed in the world but them. They were content to munch in silence without a care, dreaming. Their future was filled with adventures yet to be experienced; who had time to reflect on getting old or dying?

What do you think? She would get most of the smoked meat.

The echoing sound of young ones laughing in the woods brought back old memories to Wise-eye. "Those were the joyful days of my youth," she thought. "Travelling down river surrounded by white water. Running through the forest with my soul mate in hot pursuit. Ouch!" Multiple cramps in her leg forced her to lean back to stretch while pressing bundles of fur behind her lower back. Now was the time for Wise-eye to dream, not about the future, but her past. Her attention retreated far back in human terms to those precious, late-summer days of Wise-eye in the woods with Running-deer at their secret rendezvous.

Astor and I travelled along with the old woman's dream and witnessed every detail as we ate lots of grapes and shifted our heads periodically. At first, it was like watching two long-distance Olympians running full tilt to the finish line.

By late summer, nature had coated itself in deep green with splashes of diverse yellows and reds, temperatures still warm during the day. Heavy fog settled in on cool evenings, eliminating those pesky mosquitos along with all biting insects. On that day, the sky was clear with a southern breeze that sent ripples of blue on beaver ponds. And because of that, in shallow waters, the carp swam blind to what was above. The blue heron knew it too well.

At that point, we both read each others thought. "An excellent day to go fishing, my feathered friends." Songbirds resonated their triumphs in raising their young, finally out of the nest, if still clumsy in flight. Soon, parents, along with their siblings, would travel halfway around the world.

A time of year where a mid-day breeze could still caress bare skin. A time to cherish before the cold. Here we go. In the beginning, the couple Wise-eye and Running-deer.

fought the urge to run outdoors stark naked.

From our cloud perspective, we simply followed the bush trail with our eyes a short distance, and all sorts of information poured in regarding its function. Let me describe some of it along the way; it will give you a better idea of what was going on.

Mature growth along the path partially hid speedy chipmunks patrolling their precious territory of hazelnut bushes. The village people called it *the path of lumbering shoulders*, where natives hauled wild game over land from far away hunting grounds. At the preferred river crossing, they'd established a roadway running through the forest way up north to the sea. Where the road met the river, it was usually reasonably shallow, not too wide and with a moderate current, so it froze solid in winter. The paths were trampled knee deep in some places, and snaked, beaten smooth, along hill country. The south side, halfway down a ravine, was a strategic location for herbivores. The animals could pick up scents from downhill and spot predators approaching on all sides at a safe distance. Wolves, bears, and villagers use it constantly—it was a well-chosen roadway with the least resistance when travelling on land.

The two young lovers had exciting plans—a carefree morning. Naked, Wise-eye and her soul mate, Running-deer, took to the trail. They ran and ran along the beaten path with tree trunks rushing past their peripheral vision. Masses of tall vegetation blocked intervals of bursting sunlight on bodies in motion. Her long, black hair flew horizontally in waves, defying the laws of time and gravity. All that was missing was a piece by Beethoven in 'C" Minor playing in the background.

Millions of pointy, oval leaves overlapped each other, rolled like a green carpet on both side of the path as they ran. The scattered tree trunks on that slope were overwhelmed by them. It seemed that a populace of green leaves stood surrounding the trees in protest for some political cause, demanding, "Until we get what we want, nobody moves!"

A breathless smile widened on the young native who had the lead. "Finally, almost there," Wise-eye thought, in her forward strides. "I can see the tree." An enormous black spruce towered ahead, with future giants scattered about. It was so-so tall. The conifer stood the oldest and largest by far for miles around. Besides mountains, the century old tree presented eagles an alternative for nesting. Dried-up streaks of greyish-white splashes at the tips of the lower spruce boughs gave evidence of the birds of prey nesting ten storeys above. If a person stood to bear hug the tree trunk, his fingertips wouldn't touch by a yard and then some.

Leg-sized roots breached the soil to see daylight, only to arc back under like a hump-backed whale. Snug like bow strings, the tiny, reddish roots ran shallow along dark earth into impressive lengths. The roots spread, criss-crossing the forest floor forty meters or more from its source, the trunk. Starting from needle to finger sizes, strong and flexible, the spruce roots were gathered, debarked, and used as ropes for everyday village use.

At ground level, the three dominant roots, half exposed, curved up to form a thick base. Despite minimal sunlight, the skyscraper transformed half an acre by scattering a thick layer of acidic needles. Rustic in colour, the harsh compost and lack of sunlight discouraged vegetation, creating an alien landscape.

The dominant tree roots were spaced equally to help steady the millennium monster, a refuge for exhausted travellers in difficult weather. With the umbrella-shaped canopy, heavy rain wouldn't penetrate all the way down to its base; also, the limbs were so dense, even hailstorms gave way. Travellers could make use of the large, exposed roots as pillows. With a good sleeping blanket, the scented needles made a welcoming mattress, and the weary slept like a log until the storm passed.

What delightful years those were, from late summer to early fall; carefree adventures with Running-deer were what Wise-eye recalled. Young, subtle bodies were forgiving and quick to react. Jumping, running, and gliding with muscular legs lifting high above fallen timber. Running-deer's outstretched foot sprang in the air; would it ever touch ground again? Again, it defied the laws of the universe.

With rushing wind invading their ears, the young and the spirited lovers asked themselves, confident, "Hey! Will the birds ever keep up with us? Will the coyote dare to challenge for a race? Will the sparrow get tired and drop to the ground?" No one knew who was chasing whom, and no one cared. The controversial chipmunk showed up again, yapping like usual in the pathway. Wise-eye noticed the critter way ahead and thought to herself, "He needs to get out of the way soon. I don't want to accidentally stomp the little guy."

In a flicker, the nut cracker scattered at the last possible moment, still complaining with his tail pointing high. Wise-eye thought, "It's a good thing for the wiry chipmunk that the village boys weren't honing their hunting skills along the trail; because mister chipmunk could easily have ended up at the village fire, roasting on a stick."

While on the move, alert bodies dodged branches hanging across the trail. Periodically they stooped or side-stepped while leaning sideways to avoid being scraped by the underbrush encroaching on the path. Throughout the five-mile marathon, they revelled in lightning speed, echoing the cries of the wild. "Go-go!" Scrapes, trials, and disappointment throughout the young couple's infancy were learned, honed, and forgotten; now, as adults with skills of the woods, the arrow rarely missed the mark and their future stretched miles ahead with no end in sight. No time to die; surely a time to live, to embellish stories for the campfire, a time to dream in the present, so wishful, and so to nurture a bundle of joy in the foreseeable future.

During those years that numbered a handful, from late summer to heavy frost, the secret get-aways in the evening were what Wise-eye cherished the most. With a rolled-up Sheep skin strapped on her back, she had looked forward through tag alders branching out from the main path. Running-deer led the way with a pouch of sweet berry-water, dried fruits, and meats in his backpack plus more blankets.

Looking at the man from our cloud, Running-deer's bow with many arrows that was strung up on his back were part of him. Immediately, we understood that his conspicuous flint knife, carried on the hip, was used as a last resort in unavoidable close contact while hunting large prey. The three notches on his knife handle told how many times such an encounter had happened. Although, details of the encounters were never revealed to us, which is just as well.

While running on a carpet of dried leaves, the crunching noise released an aroma of autumn vegetation. Suddenly, the croak of a raven appeared near, yet, when tracking the source, to my astonishment Astor and I spotted a tiny cross soaring above in blue skies.

Knowing the short journey ahead made their heart glad—a five-mile run was a trifle of a burden for leg muscles accustomed to much more. "We're here." Covered with a blanket and with both arms straddling a broad root, Wise-eye lay stretched out flat on her stomach. Her elbows were bent, anchored solid into white fleece. Wise-eye's folded hands rested under her chin, motionless, as she waited with pursed lips, ready to critique what was being done to her.

The plush wool blanket had been spread out and smoothed for comfort. The edge rolling over a head size circular root, which formed as a head rest near the base of the giant tree trunk. When Wise-eye pressed her elbows over the pillow-root, it forced her spine to curve gracefully upward with her head erect, as if standing.

Both naked, her long, black hair shone silver and flowed, parting in the middle and hanging loose over the shoulders which covered her breast. Strands of long hair parted, giving way to her body contour, and continued with the ends brushing the wool blanket. Her skin appeared dark olive with a creamy glow without blemishes—the same natural complexion that skin cream companies nowadays promise with the moon.

With feminine curves flexing under her skin, arm muscles easily support her weight -- just like city folks nowadays sign up for at the gym.

Patience! It had been long enough. Wise-eye was getting restless. She hummed through her nose and then, like a spoiled child, aimlessly fiddled with a dry twig to test its strength. She snapped it in half, tossed it, and looked for a bigger one. Huff! Now she was bored. The back of her head twitched to her left as she attempted to look back. Her good side, she calls it, pertaining to the injury of her right eye. While frowning, with her mouth forming an "O" for Oh! Get serious, will you?

Lips were full, and because of her pout, no teeth were visible. When Wise-eye looked at someone with displeasure, her good eye would pierce like the arrow of a warrior.

"That's it! It's been long enough." She scowled some more with her drilling words. "No! No, you're doing it all wrong; you're dragging your knuckles again Running-deer. How many times have I told you, don't drag your knuckles. I can feel it when you do that."

Wise-eye smacked her lips reproachfully and groaned. Running-deer wasted no time, and retorted with arms waving in a defensive posture. He breathe heavily. "Okay! Let me start over." It was a silly game they played sometimes, nobody else knew. With his index finger, Running-deer drew an animal on her back, and Wise-eye had to guess what it was. If he did, it would be his turn. Nobody ever wins either, but it emptied their thoughts of the day, thoughts of the long winter ahead—for certain, a childish game, to make each other laugh.

Running-deer tightened his fist and extended his index finger that was callus and stiff from drawing too many bow strings. For him, it helped if he bit his tongue with a corkscrew face as he drew. "Focus and think hard," thought Running-deer. He started again, determined.

Moans and groans released through the nose by Wise-eye disrupted Running-deer's concentration and gave him the shakes; not good when drawing a picture. Running-deer knew without looking that her jaw would be clenched, with no room for smiling. She shifted again. How could a person concentrate on drawing when the artist's tableau fidgeted and talked back? Exasperated, he continued and finally… relief. "Okay, I'm done."

An uncomfortable silence from Wise-eye and then the chirping started. "Done already? What is that anyway, it has no form? Where did you learn to draw; is this for real? Are you sure you're done?"

Running-deer pulled back, defeated, ready to scream, his arms opened to the sky. He answered in one of his manly, defensive tone. "What do you mean, what's that? It's a living fur animal; now go on, guess what animal."

Wise-eye arms had originally supported her head, but now her hands were cupped over her ears, head hanging low. She absolutely looked distraught. Deep from within, moaning surfaced through her nose. In the silence cut short, Wise-eye replied with an even tone. "I give up; what is it?"

Thinking he had managed pretty well, Running-deer nodded. A man who preferred to fix things was now applying communication with a clue. "You can't give up now; think and consider the options, my resourceful bunny."

She answered, "No, forget it. I give up. What is it?"

The unveiling of the mysterious fur animal drawing was declared in triumph. "I just gave you a hint—a rabbit."

Nothing moved. No sounds could be heard other than the wind blowing, a squirrel chattering, crickets. Then Wise-eye's shoulder swung sideways as she faced her sketchy animal artist. Her long, black hair shifted to cover the right half of her face. Her favoured eye searched his as though to question a possible diluted mind that had zero talent in sketching animals. "Break it to him gently," she thought. The man is proud with enough ego mass to sink a canoe." With an even tone, she announced the obvious without flinching, "You hunt strange rabbits."

That did it; lightning and thunder struck. Thick muscular arms rose in protest, fingers wide apart and pointing to high heaven. Running-deer's chest expanded to expose his sensitive spot as he said, "Plunge another arrow in me if you will."

The sorrowful one had been wounded to the heart and wanted to be acknowledged by his captive; how pitiful. No response? No replies, no nurturing intentions? Engulfed in shiny, black hair, Wise-eye only stared at Running-deer with a smirk. There was such a creature as silent cruelty in the world.

"All right," said Running-deer. "I'm done with this game. Are you hungry?"

"Yes," said Wise-eye. They set themselves up for another game.

For this one, a fist with pinched fingers needed to be raised to eye level for aiming. As usual, the target was being troublesome, shaking her head and being super distractive while smiling so sweet.

Running-deer held his arm steady, concentrating on the constantly shifting target, until he finally voiced his demand. "Stop giggling and stop moving your head around like that; just hold still and open wide." Wedged between his thumb pad and index finger, a pinch of dried blueberries was rolled up in a tight ball. Hinging from the elbow, Running-deer drew his aiming hand back and forth to his cheek bone. The skillful hunter took aim—wait for it—and then released the ball in a reverse finger-snap. On each attempt, the lump of squishy dark fruit arced straight inside the mouth of Wise-eye, pluck! At this game, Running-deer was a pro, and he knew it.

Sitting cross legged, Wise-eye's body swayed backwards as the lump of fruit hit the inside of her mouth. Cheers and a burst of laughter muffled her words while chewing the juicy fruit. She swallowed quickly and then managed to say, "Wow! You are good at this, Running-deer." She tucked her waist-long hair behind her ears with her fingertips, getting ready for more.

"Ah! It's nothing," replied Running-deer. "My hunting buddies can do the same trick." He shrugged off her praise with a hand and a huff. The whole idea was to show humility, but it didn't work; she saw through him. When surrendering his feelings for her, he marvelled. As always, she twitched like a child while tucking strands behind her ear. "That woman is killing me," Running-deer thought. "She can read my thoughts before I speak, and I can't get away with anything."

The food tossing game went up a notch. Wise-eye leaned back, still sitting cross-legged with her mouth half open, mumbling challenging words. "Herre… tri… is!" It didn't make any difference; the berries went flying inside the partially opened mouth without touching her lips.

Now it was her turn to throw the juicy fruit; disaster struck. Balls of blueberries bounced all over Running-deer's nose, neck, left ear, forehead—all solid hits, except not inside the mouth. More laughter. The targeted victim had blue spots all around his face and things weren't improving.

So, the man rosed to the challenge. He wanted to put a stop to wasting food and so propped a pinecone on the ground a few feet away as a harmless target. Now Running-deer slid behind Wise-eye and saddled his bent knees around her thighs, all the while resting on his heels. The warmth of her body felt exhilarating, and he took time to adjust his body position to hers.

To restore clarity of mind, he blinked, shook his head, and then cleared his throat. A desiring breath grew passionate on the side of her neck where he knew she was ticklish to a fault. The effect was instant—she shoved his face away, followed by a lover's slap, simple for him to avoid.

"Stop,." she urged in a tone not too convincing. "Stop that and show me how to throw straight."

"Okay, look at the pinecone in front of you," said Running-deer. "Clear your mind of all thoughts and focus only on the cone." For Running-deer, this was serious stuff; they were going to solve this problem together. More delightful body adjustment as Running-deer cupped his hand under the elbow of Wise-eye for support. With the other, he held her wrist in a soft-fingered grip. He whispered softly in her ear but avoided the ticklish area. "Focus on the pinecone; think of nothing else. Now, let your arm swing free from the elbow, back and forth, back and forth like that. Now pitch and release! Keep it steady," he encouraged, "and don't let anything distract your mind until the berries are released from your fingers."

Wanting to do well for her instructor, she made an effort to straighten and adjust her posture. With a feminine hand, one swoop under her cheekbones sent strands of dark hair whipping behind on his face. The sudden brushstroke triggered a smile as he closed his eyes. With shoulders squaring up, she bit her lips and analyzed her target with one eye. Wise-eye concluded,

"After all, Running-deer is making an effort to teach me; the least I can do is give it my best."

Ready, set, one, two, aim. She swung her arm and threw… No such luck. Not even close.

Running-deer sighed. It was like teaching a turtle how to sit. Her patience to endure and learn was long spent.

Wise-eye realized she was not a natural at this throwing game and felt clumsy, therefore out it went. "Enough of this," she said, striking the air. "I'm through."

Running-deer did not argue; he didn't care one way or the other. He rolled onto his back, closed his eyes, and waited for her frustration to subside. With an extended arm, he found her knee with the tip of his fingers, a clear invitation to forget the pinecone game and come near.

In silence, Wise-eye slipped to his side, pressing for more room on the blanket. Satisfied, she propped herself up on one elbow, poking a finger in Running-deer's abs to see if she could make a dent in his chest.

Looking for trouble, are we?

Her playful posture inched closer to Running-deer's body, and she poked even more. "How can that be; is his flesh made of stone?"

Poky to the left-poky-poky in a circle?

"Let's see if flesh made of stone has feelings."

Before that experiment could take place, Running-deer sat up and growled.

Oh so, the bear with no teeth, no claws, was

ticklish. Wise-eye responded by sitting up straight, facing him. With open hands in front of her, she locked her elbows and then shoved Running-deer's upper body backwards with remarkable vigor.

Her bold action deserving merit, Running-deer threw himself backwards, arms flaring in exaggeration as though he'd been rammed by a billy-goat. With his legs already bent under him, he sprang back farther than normal. Unfortunately, the throwback resulted in a miscalculation of distance. His muscular back thudded past the sheep blanket onto hard soil covered with spruce needles. "Oof!" A sharp point penetrated his skin —a thin, dry stick. The hard ground temporary knocked the wind out of him. Without meaning to, a sharp cry of pain escaped through his mouth. His lips immediately tightened to prevent another outburst, but it was too late; she had heard.

Awash in dark hair, her naked body rose, gliding parallel to his and sweeping Running-deer's stomach with her breast. In a rush for words, she asked, "Are you okay?" Wise-eye's face was filled with concern, demanding an immediate answer.

Running deer plastered, wide-eyed grin was already established and holding. He answered in a flash. "Yes, I'm fine. I'm good, really." He wanted to preserve the heavenly atmosphere, so he wouldn't make a fuss. The feigned smile needed to be convincing, even though a devilish wood sliver under his skin throbbed with pain.

The hunger, the longing grew intense. Seeing her round face filled with happiness, the lips quivering, he thought, "No time to waste."

His leg muscles tightened as he pushed himself up to settle back on the blanket. Wise-eye helped him. Leaning past his equilibrium, Running-deer caught her halfway and continued to advance, his lips pressed to her neck. She followed, glued to his body movements as though they were one. Her hot breath on Running-deer's skin triggered shivers throughout his body.

To gain support, Running-deer shifted to roll over on the wool blanket. The finger-long dried stick embedded halfway under his skin hung loose. Tiny trickles of blood ran down his lower back. Right now, in the mind of Running-deer, he couldn't have cared less about the stick hanging from his back; it would heal.

Scattered berries from Wise-eye's throwing episode rolled down and wedged along skin folds of hips and legs. Adding warmth and friction, Running-deer and Wise-eye would be left with dark purple stains all over their lower bodies. After this was over, mingling about the village-fire would stir up busybodies to wonder. Rest assured; work will be interrupted, while making derogatory comments. What would they be thinking?

Seriously, Running-deer and Wise-eye didn't care. The rush was on. In that moment, two hearts could fly on wings like eagles. In time, you have lover's quarrels, but not tonight. Tonight, the moon hung low, casting shadows over nature that stood.

Perched high above a neighbouring spruce, the grey owl twisted his head, looked down, and hooted at the mishmash of arms and legs crossing each other in the moonlight. Exhaustion had caught up with the young lovers, who were now engulfed in tomorrow's sweet dreams.

Not far over the hill, the silver fox slept snug in his den, a head buried in a puff of fur, eyes shut, with folded ears twitching at times, followed by the eyebrows. Mister fox was also in the middle of a dream —a wonderful love-dream. Tomorrow foxy will discover a secret valley filled with many rabbits that grew no legs.

While her thoughts returning to the present, Wise-eye observed with curiosity her granddaughter flitting from one tree truck to another on trailing legs plowing fluffy snow. "Her handsome canoe paddler is persistent," she thought, "and righteous to the sea and back; he wants what was stolen from him, a strip of smoked meat." As she craned her neck to see them disappear headlong in deep snow, the growls of the abductor and the cries of the captured resonated across the valley floor.

Sitting erect like a queen on her Dall sheep blanket, the old woman gazed afar to the east. Her eyes sparkled even more. With pursed lips and a twinkle in her eye, Wise-eye could not help but wonder, "Does my granddaughter also have secret games?"

Another Killing Zone

Without a word from our guardian angel except a nod with one arm extended, Astor and I were thrown into another killing zone. Without even asking our permission. Just like that, pouf! We found ourselves standing between native men guarding the packing trail. A week had passed since the large moose was cut up and transported by sled to the village. The hunt for large prey never let up in the winter. Just hours prior, a good-sized wood caribou was taken down near the river. The only thing different was the presence of dogs pulling empty toboggans and no desperation in their strides because this time, people were not starving.

I grew a bit tense when I heard a sound resounding loud through the forest.

The wolves were howling. They'd caught the scent of the caribou killed by the villagers and recognized the sigh of scavengers gathering in the trees. Throughout the forest, lower boughs were blanketed white with no fencing, and no gates that could be shut. The native hunters knew it well and were ready for possible four-legged intruders towing an appetite. They stood an arrow shot from each other, circling the killing site, with more guards scattered along the packing trail. With an arm stretched to one side, that is how a hunter readied his bow. For now, the grip was loose, and a flint arrow rested on the shaft with the index finger curled on top.

Along with shallow breathing, their minds were born to see through the forest, ears seasoned to detect a mouse scratching under snow. Their physical status would best be described as slim and firm; therefore, the crunching sounds under their snowshoes when stepping forward were faint. One of them turned to the other and gestured with his chin, "Look, look up over the hill in the underbrush; are those shadows or beasts?" The distinction could be minute. Nonetheless, there cannot be any disasters. The wolves would not have their way with hind quarters or any meat at all. On that watch, the grandson of Running-deer, the one who doesn't waste arrows to kill, is among them.

Astor and I never witnessed what happened during the last part of that day. Did the wolves attack some group hauling the wood caribou meat? Only the angels knew the outcome. The two of us were hopeful that by the grace of God, the people triumphed and managed to transport all the meat to their village without wolf interference.

After that, I believe we left the area. Ump. Or did we…?

Back at the House

An outside voice jerks at my subconscious, and I am cut off.

"Then what happened Dad?" I found myself lounging in my son's lazy-boy chair in the same position that a was an hour ago, and Diane was sitting on the chair with Lillian fast asleep in her lap.

I still trail the haunted cobwebs from another world. I jolted, groaning like an old man with a stiff neck. (Okay, I'm an old man with a stiff neck.) "What?" I hold up my hands.

My son grasps the arms of his chair. "The village story, Dad. Did the wolves get through and ate the caribou meat?"

Feeling disoriented, I sit in silence, my mouth half open, and manage, "No, like I said, I do not think so? Most of the meat got through, I think." My mind honestly draws a blank. "Oh, I just told you, we left before we could find out."

My son raises his vocal cords like schoolteachers sometimes do, clearly impatient. "Are you with us? Did you forget your medication?"

Not that again. I scream inside and make a point of him seeing my eyes roll up to the ceiling.

Diane glances at Finnegan, critical. The gesture made him realize his affront, so he lowers his eyes in a sheepish smile.

I finally slip out of my trance completely. The half-empty coffee cup tips dangerously on my lap, although the contents are now cold. In a state of reverie, I must have rubbed the rim with my thumb for hours, until it hurt. After so many years, I have lived through the heavenly encounter once more. Like a pirate returning to his empty treasure chest in a cave. I felt the chill, I heard the drip-drip, and for what? The chest is empty. I can't relive the past; it's gone forever.

Travelling at lightning speed without "G' forces on a sofa cloud, with no wind in my ears. I wouldn't be included next time; my guardian angel said so. Was I being selfish? I'd gotten my blessing forty-nine years ago.

This is not the end of the story, only the beginning. Although, things will not be exactly the same as before. Like the French saying, *"Passer le baton."* Should I play it safe and leave Finnegan and Diane with this interesting heavenly encounter story of interacting with nature? Unique lessons to learn in life? Or, I could lean in a different direction. Why should I share the rest? It's like the story in the Bible, where a man finds a priceless treasure in a field. He doesn't tell a soul, but goes out and purchases the land where the jewels were found.

It's way past my afternoon nap. I want to be that

man—secretly buy the field and go home. And then I think about Jonah and the whale. I feel like I'm between a rock and a hard place. What to do?

As I ponder my situation, Finnegan speaks again. This time, the voice is truly softened in my loving boy. "Can I get you another cup of coffee, Dad?"

Shrivelled in posture like a pheasant on a ten-day pilgrimage, I stare at my cup, away somewhere. My voice helps me trek forward. "Yes," I say. "That would be lovely."

My servant son hurries back. "Do you take cream, Father?" The prompting was filled with pleasantries.

I felt special and encouraged, so I ask," Do you have any more Baileys?"

Remain seated, I will complete my story to the full, only this time with the replenished aroma of hot coffee mixed with Baileys, and yes, cookies.

The Apparition

"We came back in the same body position that we'd left two hours earlier, sitting under the shaded tree. Unknown to me at the time, my eyes had stayed open the whole time. I knew that because my binoculars were still lightly resting on my cheek bones."

Half gesturing, I hold imaginary field glasses to my face.

"After the initial shock, I cannot believe what I had just experienced, not totally grasping that my two hours on a cloud in the sky with Astor were over.

"I pulled back as if I had touched a hot potato tied around my neck. The binoculars bounced and settled to my stomach. By then, a racket had invaded our space, a mixture of growling and high-pitched wincing. From a distance, straight ahead of us on our side of the river, the disturbance was evident. Wolves were dispersing through the grassy forest like thieves with their plan accomplished in record time. With the moose rack leaning low in swampy grass, the result was obvious. The giant beast that had confronted the seven wolves had been overwhelmed hours before and devoured by the pack. All around the killing site, the smell of fresh blood soaked the forest floor. Even small creatures like the squirrels kept silent, as if in mourning or still weary."

Time to take a breather. I reached over and set my cup on the coffee table so I can lean back. My neck muscles loosen as I sank my head onto soft leather. Now I can breathe more thoughtfully; and finish the story for my glued audience. I pause and draw silent. My hands lift from the armchair as a deliberate gesture to hold on. I begin cautiously to reveal the main purpose for my story. That's when I become obedient in the eyes of God, so I don't end up inside the stomach of a fish like Jonah in the Bible; and my conclusion has nothing to do with Baileys in the coffee or forgetting my medication. I continue.

After Astor's second backslap, which I did not feel either, he said, "Finally, the time has arrived, Joe. I'm heading for my favourite fishing spot where I was last year. Take your time, follow me when ready, there's no rush."

At first, I hesitated and stood for twenty minutes scanning the clouds around me. I felt relieved when the flaming window in the sky had disappeared. Also, no angels were walking over treetops. I lowered my head, to see Astor disappear under thick underbrush in the direction of the river. I could not hold my suspense any longer and became anxious to discuss the sofa-cloud experience with our angel guide, and see if the two angels were still around somewhere, even though the opening in the sky was gone.

As I started walking forward cautiously, I realized that Astor had been prudent enough to detour around the ambushed moose site, even after the wolves had left. I found my fishing guide all right, right where I knew he would be from describing his precious fishing hole on the road. A lone dead cedar marked King Fisher Island at the river's edge. From up-river, a drum-sized tree had washed ashore on the pebble beach. Half of the water-logged beam tapered down to the river and sank under the current. On land, the huge base of the log was dry as a bone and half buried. Astor was stretched out on top of it, snoring, the Australian hat over his face. I was puzzled. No idea why he wasn't standing at the river fishing.

Instinctively, I swung my head to look around. A stone's throw away downriver, the short one stood there —well, shorter compared to the other angel. I couldn't believe my eyes at the time; the angel was holding Astor's fishing rod and casting across the river as if everything was normal. I had to pinch myself. Nothing changed. The angel (the one lower to the ground) was still there fishing and Astor still snoring.

After hearing the croaks of a large bird in the sky, I looked up and saw the raven gliding in a circle as if confused. I felt the connection and spoke out loud. My exasperation echoed across the river. "I understand," I said. "My mind is doing circles too!" I got dizzy and swayed as I stood there perspiring. I found my legs again and sneaked over next to Astor. He lay there stretched out on the log with his legs crossed at the ankles, I gave him a kick, and prayed for a touch of normality.

He woke up, fumbling for his precious Australian hat sliding to the ground. He looked at me, irritated, as if I had punched him in the face. Not a bad idea, I thought at the time; seeing actual blood on a man's lip, and confirming that a warm-blooded human is still on this earth. That was when he growled at me, "What? Why did you wake me? The pain in my head is getting worse."

I had no idea what pain he was talking about, and I didn't care. I stretched out my arm to get his undivided attention, the angel. "right-right over there." I whispered between clenched teeth. "There's an angel fishing with your rod."

Astor glanced at the angel that was preoccupied with his casting technique, and then back at me, his forehead wrinkled in pain. "Yes, I know. I lent it to him."

Exasperated, I asked, "What for?"

A disoriented look crossed his face again, while rubbing the back of his neck. Without a second thought, he said. "So, he could go fishing."

I nearly screamed. "Does God know about this situation?" I did not wait for Astor's reply, I spoke out loud to heaven, and my words stretched out across the river. "Okay, hold on. I'm cool with that," I said. "I can play along with this game." With a touch of sarcasm, I spoke to Astor, and I spoke to the Universe, "I didn't know that angels like to fish!"

Astor shook his head. "Not all angels, only Eagle-feather. That's his name."

My arms opened wide, conceding defeat. "That's nice to know," I said as I walked towards the buck-skinned angel. Halfway there, I turned around to ask Astor, "Does Eagle-feather talk?"

"When fishing, not so much," replied Astor.

Right. Now I was standing next to the guardian-looking angel called Eagle-feather. I narrowed my eyes to question myself. Does he look like one of the men who had winched our truck when we got stuck in the mud? No, I must be feverish, it couldn't be. I braced myself just in case I disappeared in a cloud of smoke; I had read in The Dead Sea Scrolls that angels are powerful beings.

After I'd stood there for a while, mesmerized, I felt at peace and decided to present the angel with a miracle test. After all, this is how the bible instructs Christian's; test everything to make sure that it comes from God. Crossing my arms while basking in a certain air of defiance, I said, "On your next cast pull in a three-foot salmon, if you can."

He did. Huh. Not bad. I was not satisfied yet, so I ask again. "Now, on your next cast, pull in a four-foot salmon."

He did it, this time with a smirk on his face. Hold on a minute. Then I provided our angel the ultimate challenge. "Now reel in a smaller fish with a gold coin in his mouth."

Eagle-feather paused, breathed in heavily, lowered his head and turned to me. "Sorry, only the Father can pull that one off."

Now it was my turn to have a smirked face, satisfied. After fishing alongside Eagle-feather for an hour, I made a rough calculation in my head so as not to exceed our limit. We caught two more good-sized fish for the truck's cooler. I started filleting fish and left the heads for foxes.

Astor was preoccupied with the other tall angel, organizing a day camp. They walked along the riverbank searching for kindling and gathering round stones for the fire pit. The two were talking together like they were old friends. Astor kept looking towards us as if waiting for something to happen; and then it came. Eagle-feather leaned over and said to me, right out of the blue, "You need to pray for Astor."

Stunned, I replied with a highly intellectual human response. "Huh?"

Once more, Eagle-feather leaned sideways, and repeated his request in a calm, nurturing voice. "You need to pray for Astor's tumor, Joe. It gives him migraine headaches. Doctors cannot remove the tumor because the mass will cause irreparable damage to his brain. As you can imagine, at present, he cannot enjoy life to the full."

I recovered some and said, "Oh!" Silenced followed. Thinking-thinking. "Why don't you pray for him?" I said, after pondering the situation. "With those fat sword knives attached to your waist, don't you have a more intimate relationship with God?"

Not true, I lied; I only thought about the fat sword part.

"No can do," said Eagle-feather. You also have an intimate relation with God, and only humans can pray for each other." He cast his line into the river. "Besides, we made an agreement ten years ago, Astor and me. He lets me fish with his rod for a few hours every year, and I arrange for healing if he ever gets a life-threatening sickness."

Stumped by the plan, I felt leery of simply jumping in to pray for a cure. I felt like St. Peter walking on water—I needed a steady hand for my predicament, as I was sinking fast. I performed my not-me dance as I pleaded like Moses in the bible did. "Why me? I'm not good at praying. After a short period, my mind goes blank, my speech is poor, and the words don't come out right. I have a better idea; pick one of your angel friends. I'm certain—"

"Shush," said Eagle-feather. "I think I'm getting a bite. No." He grunted in disappointment. "False alarm." After casting down river, the angel turned severely to me this time. While reeling in, he stared at me without blinking. "Didn't I make myself clear? Only humans can pray for each other, and there are no humans around except you. So, get going, will you? You're encroaching on my fishing time." Eagle-feather made another cast, this time almost across to the other bank.

Thinking, "He must have a good left hook," shaken, I wiped my brow with an open hand, and then swallowed hard and walked gingerly back to Astor. He was sitting around a blazing campfire with the other, towering angel that hardly spoke. I had no idea how in God's name I would do this.

My knees shook, walking circles around the campfire bought me some time, and my mind went blank several times. In the end, though, I did it. I laid hands on Astor's head, praised God, acknowledged His holy name on earth as it was in heaven, and asked God to heal the tumor that had invaded Astor's body.

Grace

"What more needs to be said? The man was healed instantly. Not by me but through the power of the Holy Spirit in me. You must have read about Astor the fishing guide in the paper when he died—the oldest living person in Canada, 115 years. I suspect the Holy Spirit fine-tuned his organs to make him live that much longer. Bonus! God's grace overflows all the time."

I lean back in the armchair. "Now it's almost here again."

Finnegan tilts his head, his brow furrowed. "What's almost here?" Diane raises her head to, and a pencil rolls to the floor. Lillian is out for the night, so I thought.

In a tense voice, I reply, "The jubilee, 50 years."

"What does a jubilee have to do with your story, Dad?"

I let the question hang in the air for a moment before dropping the bomb. "It could very well have to do with my life or death."

You could've heard a feather drop in the living

room. I broke the silence in the ultimate race to prolong my life. "The jubilee happens to fall on this coming Sunday. I hope there's no pack of wolves this time. Either way, would you and your family like to skip church and go fishing on Sunday? It could be a life-changer for Lillian. Come together as a family and see for yourselves what I have been talking about," I said. "We have nothing to lose and everything to gain."

Finnegan and Diane stare at each other, dumb-founded. As I wait for their answer, Lillian jumps on my lap, her face glowing. "Take me fishing with the angels, Grandpa. I want to go."

I throw my head back and cheer out loud at her request. Ow, ow! I must stop Lillian from jumping on my knees with her bent legs. I'm getting too old for that, and her much too heavy.

Jubilee

Sunday morning dawns clear with no clouds. Finnegan is driving his 4X4 pickup truck. I am in the passenger seat with my window open, elbow resting on the frame as I stick out my arm, the wind whistling through my fingers. Diane and Lillian sit in the back, their faces pressed to the window.

I point at the sky, and all three of their heads swivel to look. An eagle soars high above us, enjoying the view as the crow flies. Dust rolls behind the truck, forming a white cloud that gradually dissipates in the eastern breeze.

A country song blares on the radio. "On the Road Again." I smile. Whatever the day might bring, I am, in this moment, completely at peace.

A logging truck whizzes by with its horn blaring. "Going fishing with my family." The lyrics have been changed again.

The raven is nowhere to be seen.

Acknowledgments

Having an idea and turning it into a book is as hard as it sounds. The experience is both internally challenging and rewarding. I especially want to thank the individuals that helped make this a reality. Complete thanks to my devoted wife, Claire, for her unwavering support with a mountain of patience. Also, my editor and Christian friend, Sara Davison. Thank you for your expertise, guidance and, like you said, "we need to tie up loose ends." And there were many, many loose ends.